FICTION HOUSE PRESS
PRESENTS

VANGUARD SCIENCE FICTION

June 1958
Vol. 1, No. 1

This reprint edition is a facsimile of the original pulp magazine. Variations in printing and quality can be attributed to the original magazine which was printed on rough woodpulp paper. No attempt has been made to politically correct any language deemed inappropriate to the modern reader.

ISBN 978-1-64720-400-6

www.FictionHousePress.com
fictionhousepress@gmail.com

VANGUARD
science fiction

Vol. I, No. 1 June, 1958

Novelettes

Short Stories

Features

VANGUARD SCIENCE FICTION, Vol. I, No. 1, is published bi-monthly by Vanguard Science Fiction, Inc., 50 Overlook Terrace, New York 33, N. Y. Single copy is 35 cents. Subscription 20 issues $6.00. Copyright 1958 by Vanguard Science Fiction, Inc. Application pending for entry as second class matter at the post office New York, N. Y. Editorial address: 703 Nostrand Ave., Brooklyn 16, N. Y. The publishers assume no responsibility for unsolicited material. Please enclose a stamped, self-addressed envelope with all submitted material. All stories printed in this magazine are fiction, any similarity between the characters and actual persons is purely coincidental. Printed in the U.S.A. All subscriptions should be sent to Vanguard Science Fiction, Box 188, Planetarium Station, New York 24, N. Y. Editor James Blish, Publisher Larry Schecter.

Cover by ED EMSH *illustrating* S.O.S. PLANET UNKNOWN,
Drawing for the TALES THEY TELL, *by Kelly Freas.*

IN THE BEGINNING

Picking a name for a new science fiction magazine is a tough job, especially if you're trying to avoid duplicating any of the 60-odd names that have already been used. We were happy with Vanguard, however, particularly because it suggested the Earth Satellite Project, which we were then thinking of as man's first real step into space.

Then came the epochal announcements of October 4, November 3 and November 7, and Project Vanguard abruptly became Project Offguard. People who knew about our magazine promptly began calling us to ask whether or not we planned to change the name.

As you can see, we decided against it. To be sure, the associations with the American satellite project are now a dubious asset; but we are not really in the satellite business. The name also suggests that the magazine hopes to push to the fore in its field. That is still our hope—so the name stands.

We hope to print authentic science fiction: the pure stuff, of which we have seen all too little in recent years. Everyone has his own definition of what "the pure stuff" means. We subscribe to Theodore Sturgeon's:

A good science-fiction story is a story with a human problem, and a human solution, which would not have happened at all without its science content.

Damon Knight has suggested that "speculative content" might be a better term than "science content", but speculation in a void is not for us. We would like to see the speculation in the story backed by a plausible rationale. If the hero glows green and doesn't have to eat or breathe, for instance, we would like to see these facts explained. We won't accept them simply as "givens", nor are we going to be satisfied with a token explanation ("'Aha, I thought so,' Dr. Zorki said. 'Radioactive DDT.'")

The fact that the most successful magazine in this field prints the highest proportion of stories of this kind (though not as many as it used to) indicates to us that most science fiction readers share our preference for the genre. It is that preference, and that audience, that Vanguard hopes to satisfy.

Vanguard is first and foremost a fiction magazine. Except for L. Sprague de Camp's regular column and Lester del Rey's book reviews (both exclusive to us), we will be devoting our pages to stories.

We may print letters, if you write us some interesting ones. Primarily, however, we are in business to print stories—and, as an earnest of good intentions, we plan no editorials for future issues.

—JAMES BLISH

SPOKEN

707

SIOBHAN McKENNA: IRISH VERSE AND BALLADS. The celebrated actress, star of The Chalk Garden, Saint Joan and The Rope Dancers, reads Irish verse with surpassing loveliness; poems by William Butler Yeats, ballads, folksongs and lyrics by James Joyce, James Stephens and others.

705

AN INFORMAL HOUR WITH S. J. PERELMAN. The one and only S. J. Perelman brings to your ear such classics as And Thou Beside Me, Yacketing in the Wilderness; The Sweeter the Tooth, the Nearer the Couch; and Is There an Osteosynchrondroitrician in the House!

721

AN INFORMAL HOUR WITH ERSKINE CALDWELL. The internationally known writer reading four of his most colorful short stories: Where the Girls Were Different, A Small Day, The People v. Abe Lathan, Colored and It Happened Like This.

745

ANN MORAY: GAELIC SONGS AND LEGENDS. These songs have a strange beauty, a very definite physiognomy and a very definite soul. The melodies are as purely perfect as melodies can be, and are narrated and sung to perfection in the native idiom of the singer's homeland.

716

AN INFORMAL HOUR WITH J. B. PRIESTLEY. Who reads his essays on "Delight" (including Smoking in a Hot Bath, Long Trousers, The Mineral Water in Bedrooms of Foreign Hotels) in precisely the manner you would expect that has made him famous here and abroad.

726

AN INFORMAL HOUR WITH DOROTHY PARKER. When she reads her story Horsie, and recites her bitter-sweet poems, you will be thrilled to have included inimitable Dorothy Parker among your guests!

Here's what the critics have to say about SPOKEN ARTS: *Thomas Lask* in THE NEW YORK TIMES says: . . ."seems to be doing in a more comprehensive manner what most other companies have done only sporadically . . . the records can be enjoyed in the quiet of the living room, but it occurred to this listener that they would fit in nicely in discussion groups, classrooms, forums and the like." *Edward Tatnall Canby*, in HARPER'S says: . . ."If this is a sample I am enthusiastic . . . the real thing, and tops of their kind." *John M. Conly*, in HIGH FIDELITY says: . . ."Unalloyed delights." *Irving Kolodin*, in THE SATURDAY REVIEW says: . . . "thanks should be in order for the recording venture called SPOKEN ARTS . . . intimate . . . beautifully focused sound."

ALL RECORDS $5.95 EACH

ARTS

710

GOLDEN TREASURY OF JOHN BETJEMAN. "Mr. Betjeman is one of the most original poets now writing. Their (the poems') metrical skill, their wit, their sharp observation, all delight the reader; these poems are in a peculiar degree memorable." The Spectator

733

THE GEORGICS OF VIRGIL. Translated and read by the English poet, C. Day Lewis, this Latin masterpiece startles us by its freshness and timeless lyrical quality.

734

POEMS OF T. S. ELIOT. The Waste Land created a revolution in modern poetry and will remain as a classic of the 20th Century. It is read by Robert Speaight, Eliot's noted associate and interpreter .

703

DR. FRANK C. BAXTER. From the University of Southern California, Dr. Baxter's "campus" has spread all over the country. Here in "The Nature of Poetry" you understand why he is considered one of the great creative teachers of our day.

714

DR. ROBERT M. HUTCHINS. The former President of the University of Chicago, now head of the Fund for the Republic, shows his brilliance as an educator in this discussion on "The Promise of Education."

704

ARTHUR MILLER. The Pulitzer prize winner in a provocative discussion of attitudes towards character portrayal, with readings from his "Death of a Salesman" and "The Crucible."

LAWRENCE COMPANY
Box 1708, Grand Central Station
New York 17, N. Y.

☐ Please send me the following $5.95 records. My check or money order is enclosed.

Numbers: ______ ______ ______ ______ ______ ______

☐ Please send me the complete catalog of SPOKEN ARTS releases.

Name..

Address...

City.....................................*Zone*..........*State*....................................

SOS, PLANET

She died slowly, and her people fought for her life—and for their own lives—to the very end. It was like, almost, the inevitable death of a human being from old age—the breakdown of one function after another, culminating in the final, lethal convulsions. Yet she was not old, as men measure the age of their ships. She was just ... unlucky. The minor, undetectable flaws resulting from careless workmanship during her building, the other flaws introduced during routine repairs and overhauls had all, somehow, conspired in a snowballing effect and sequence of breakdowns and disasters to kill her.

Most of her people died with her —slashed to ribbons when the madly spinning flywheels of the Mannschenn Drive unit shrugged off the makeshift, jury-rigged controls (the controls proper had been destroyed by the fire some few days earlier); or asphyxiated when the shards of jagged metal, impelled by the centrifugal force of the exploding gyroscopes, sliced through airtight bulkheads and shell plating. Two more had died of their own success in repairing her five emergency venturis, when, by one of those failures of coordination to which men are prone when their environment is disintegrating, the rockets were test-fired while the troubleshooters were still outside. Their deaths, it subsequently turned out, had been for nothing; the plasma tanks had sprung, allowing most of the reaction mass for the rockets to evaporate into space. There was no longer enough left to move her usefully.

Only one officer — the assistant purser—survived; he had been on

It was a curiously Earth-like world the castaways found — and like Earth, its real savagery was hidden.

UNKNOWN

by

A. Bertram Chandler

his way from the control room to the engine room with a message, the intercommunication system having broken down. Seven passengers survived—shut in one miraculously unholed section of the ship by the slamming emergency airtight doors.

Kennedy was the assistant purser's name—Ralph Kennedy. He was a tall young man, skinny rather than slim, with a high bridged, bony nose, fair hair that tended to recede at the temples, ears that protruded more than slightly. The horn-rimmed spectacles—he would not wear contact lenses—magnified his rather pale grey eyes. It may have been his uniform that now lent him his air of command—then, again, it may not. This much is certain—he was meeting this major crisis with a coolness that he had not, until this instant, known that he possessed.

He was, by virtue of his rank, king—king of a little world that was a wedge shaped segment of a disc seventy five feet in diameter, ten feet in thickness. He had reason to suppose that the rest of the disc—as well as of the rest of the ship, of which the disc was only a small part—was uninhabitable. The fact that the automatic doors had shut argued that there was hard vacuum on the other side of them.

He stood there, swaying slightly, the magnetized soles of his shoes holding him to the deck, waiting for his subjects to say their say, to make their petitions. He looked at them—the four men, the three women. He wondered if he looked as frightened as they did. He thought, I should look more frightened. Theirs is the fear of the unknown—mine is the fear of the known. And what I know is worse than any imaginings.

It was Major Fuller who broke the silence. He thrust his corpulent body to the forefront of the little knot of passengers, demanded, as he would have demanded an explanation from some erring N.C.O., "What's happened? Hey, young man, what's happened?"

"I think," said Kennedy cautiously, "that it's the Mannschen Drive unit. You've all seen it, of course—that affair of spinning, precessing gyroscopes right in the heart of the ship. The controls of it were giving trouble. They must have failed. Metal—the metal of the flywheels—can stand just so much. When the revolutions exceeded a certain limit the wheels either broke from their bearings, or exploded."

"How do you know it wasn't the Pile?" barked the Major. "Shouldn't you be checking for radio-activity?"

"If it had been the Pile," said Kennedy, "we shouldn't be discussing it. Besides, you will notice that the emergency, battery-powered lights aren't burning; we're still using current drawn directly from the Pile."

"Who's in charge?" snapped Fuller.

"I am, Major."

"What! A mere purser's pup!"

"That will do," said Kennedy sharply. "I want you all to know that I am in charge of this section until relieved by somebody senior to myself. It may well be that I am in charge of the ship—or what's left of her. If anybody here has experience or qualifications that will make him more suitable for the job . . ."

There was silence.

Fuller would have liked to have stepped forward, thought Kennedy, but he hasn't the guts. After all—he's Commissariat, not Combat. Gladen could, perhaps, but he's too lazy. He'll be content to write a novel around this incident when—or if—we're rescued. (And yet, Kennedy reminded himself, Gladen had been, once, Second Mate of a trading schooner on Procyon III, or Atlantia, as the colonists call it. It wouldn't pay to underrate that experience now.) Tolliver will never dare say boo to any authority—he's too much of a mouse, too much under the thumb of that big, fat wife of his. And Grant, like all newly married men, wants just to

---

A. BERTRAM CHANDLER is the pen-name of a British seaman far better known by this name (which first appeared in science fiction in 1944) than by his own. Chandler is also almost alone among well-known s-f writers in that he has yet to produce a novel; but one of his longest stories, "Giant Killer," is an acknowledged classic.

sit in a corner and hold hands with *his* wife. The women? Mrs. Tolliver—the typical, suburban housewife. . . . Mrs. Grant—not one yet, but she will be (if she's lucky enough to come through this).... Miss Weldon—what use will a dress designer be in a lifeboat?

"So I take it," said Kennedy, "that nobody wants my job. All right. I'll tell you what I'm going to do. I'm going to get a spacesuit out of the locker, and I'm going to use the suit radio to see if there's anybody else alive in the ship—the Drive Unit's not working now, so that'll be possible. Then I'm going out into the axial shaft and going through the ship, looking for survivors. I'll find out if any of the boats are still usable at the same time. I'll try to find out where we are."

"You're leaving us here," said Mrs. Tolliver, her voice accusatory.

"Somebody has to go," said Kennedy.

"And somebody should go with you," remarked Gladen quietly. "I'll be pleased to—after all," he added, grinning mirthlessly, "it's all material."

"How many times have I heard *that,* Stephen?" asked Miss Weldon.

"You don't have to listen," replied the writer. "Now, Kennedy, I suggest that after we get suited up, somebody – what about you, Susan?—puts on a helmet to keep in radio touch with us. We can report on what we find, and if we get into trouble we can yell for help. Doubtless Major Fuller will lead the charge to our rescue."

"There's no need to be funny, Gladen," barked Fuller.

"Was I being funny, Fuller? If I wasn't, it doesn't say much for your military reputation."

"Let's get these suits on," said Kennedy.

He went to the locker that stood in the alleyway, pulled out three of the stiff suits. One he handed to Gladen, the other he got into himself. Then, before putting on his own helmet, he showed Miss Weldon how to operate the tiny radio in the helmet of the third suit. He was amused by the contrast—the ugly, utilitarian headpiece topping her slim elegance. She guessed his thoughts, smiled at him through the thick, transparent plastic. He saw her lips moving, but heard nothing.

He put on his own helmet.

"If anybody saw me *now,*" he heard her say, "they'd know that I wasn't a *hat* designer."

"Your hair," he said, "looks better without a hat, anyhow."

"Come off it, young Kennedy," Gladen's voice crackled in the helmet speaker. "This is no time to be praising our Susan's auburn tresses."

"No," agreed Kennedy. "It's not." He raised his voice slightly. "Kennedy here, assistant purser. I am in Section Nine, Segment A. There are eight of us here—seven passengers and myself. Is there anybody else . . . alive? Come in, please. Come in."

He repeated the message a second time, and a third.

"It looks as though we're the only ones," said Gladen gravely.

"Looks like it," he said quietly, "We're going out now, Miss Weldon. We'll keep you informed."

"Do just that," she replied.

The little airlock leading into the axial shaft reminded Kennedy unpleasantly of a coffin. And yet, when he was through into what was left of the ship, he regretted having left its cramping confines. Space is so vast and a ship is so small—and when that ship is no more—as Gladen phrased it—than a drifting colander space seems vaster still. Here and there, in the twisted alleyways, lights were still burning—but they were dim and pale against the stars that gleamed through the rents in the tortured metal. And there was a sun ahead of them—neither of the men could see it directly yet but its glare struck through the pierced hull, was reflected aft from bright metal surfaces.

Kennedy and Gladen made a methodical search. They pulled themselves aft along the axial shaft and then, section by section, worked their way forward. They learned, quite early, that it was better to ignore the bodies. Some of them had been ripped or smashed, others burst by their own rapidly expanding internal pressure. None of them was pretty.

They came at last to the control room—or what was left of it. With the darkest filters of their helmets in place, they stared for a while at the glaring sun, at the planet that showed slightly to one side of it.

"What star is it?" asked Gladen at last.

"I don't know," admitted Kennedy. "The ship was not in normal space-time until the Drive blew up—and the explosion might have thrown us anywhere or, even, anywhen. As you see—the automatic log and the three dimensional charts have been destroyed. And the computor. If that were working we could feed what data we have into it and get some sort of an answer."

"What's this?" asked the writer. "A sextant—although not quite the kind that I was used to on Atlantia. I wonder if I can use it wearing a spacesuit . . ."

He took the instrument out of its case, held it as close to his eye as the helmet would permit. He looked at the reading. He raised the sextant to his eye again, his gloved fingers working clumsily on the micrometer. Again he checked the reading.

He said, "It's time we were getting out of here. The way the diameter of that sun's increasing, we're falling into it – and not slowly, either. That planet *may* be capable of supporting life."

"The boat in the Section Seven blister was intact," said Kennedy. "Miss Weldon! Tell the passengers to get into their suits and to prepare to abandon ship! We'll be back for them in a few minutes."

"I'll tell them," said Susan Weldon. "I'll tell them. But I don't anticipate any wild enthusiasm."

There was not, as Susan Weldon had forecast, any wild enthusiasm. The Grant couple actually said they were prepared to stay in wreck until picked up—Kennedy had to explain, in words of one syllable, firstly that the wreck was falling into the sun and secondly that it would be impossible to get out a distress signal until the boat was out and clear from the ship. He did not add that the chances of the signal's being picked up by any vessel capable of reaching them in less than a matter of years were remote in the extreme.

Then, both Gladen and the girl were inclined to be too bossy, too inclined to try to prevent the others from transferring their most cherished treasures from their cabins to the boat. Kennedy intervened. "The boat," he said, "is officially capable of carrying sixty people. We shall be landing on an unknown world—we may find that it is one of our colonies, on the other hand we may find that it has never even been surveyed. Anything—but anything—could be useful."

"Then I'll bring my typewriter and a supply of paper," said Gladen.

"Why not?"

"And I'll bring my portable electric sewing machine," said Susan Weldon.

"Oh, and could I bring my washing machine?" asked Mrs. Tolliver. "It's in the baggage hold, I was taking it for our new house on Caranthia . . ."

"No," said Kennedy. "We have no time to lose. The stuff in cabins doesn't matter, but we can't afford to scour the ship for extras. Into your spacesuits now, all of you. As soon as you're sealed I'm going to open both airlock doors."

"Do as the man says," added Gladen. He seemed to be extracting enjoyment from the situation.

Kennedy fumed and fidgetted while the passengers got suited up. They were so *slow*. Neither he nor Gladen had been able to compute the rate of the vessel's fall into the sun of this planetary system, but the purser knew that there was no extreme emergency on that score. What did have him worried was the distinct possibility that the ship would collide with the planet that they had seen, the planet to which he intended to take the lifeboat.

At last the passengers were ready, and Kennedy made a rapid but thorough inspection of each of the spacesuits. He had done this sort of thing often enough at boat drills, but had never dreamed that the day would come when he would have to do it in, as he put it to himself, playing-for-keeps circumstances.

When he was satisfied he went to the little airlock, broke the seals on the valves and opened them. Then he was able to open both the doors.

With Gladen's and Susan Weldon's help he organized the people into a human conveyor belt—it was easier loading the boat that way than having everybody struggling through the axial shaft loaded with his own personal possessions. He felt happier when he had all the survivors into the boat and the doors dogged tight. He allowed himself to hope that the boat had not been afflicted by the same curse as had been the mother ship—and was harsh with Tolliver when he voiced the same thought.

The launching of the boat was automatic. Kennedy waited until the passengers were all strapped into their seats, made sure that his own belt was properly adjusted, then pressed the red launching button. For a second he thought that there was something amiss—perhaps there was—and then the rockets fired. He was slammed back into the padding and inflicted a painful bite on his tongue.

He remembered all that he had learned at the Academy. He exerted his strength, raised his hand against the acceleration, cut the Drive. He wasted no time, as the others were doing, in heaving grateful sighs of relief at the return to the comfort of free fall. His first job, his most important job, was to get himself oriented.

The ship was still close, but was receding visibly. Looking at her, Kennedy was surprised that anybody had survived. She reminded him of a journey that he had made through desert country on one of his holidays, when he had seen, and shuddered at the sight, the bleached bones, picked clean of all flesh, of migrating animals that had failed to make it to the next water hole and had perished of thirst. Not only was the ship dead but, with her shell plating torn away and her structural members exposed, she was like a skeleton.

The sun was right astern. Kennedy adjusted the viewport dimmers, then actuated the gyroscope to swing the boat. Soon he was able to pick out the planet—of the apparent size of a melon, it was. He fired the rockets again, killing the velocity of the boat away from the not very distant world. He said, to nobody in particular, "The automatic pilot can do the rest, until we hit atmosphere."

There was one thing left to do.

The assistant purser pressed the button that would put the automatic radio distress call out. He waited until it had been sending for ten minutes, then switched to manual. His gloved hand was not too clumsy on the key.

"S O S," he sent. "S O S. Survivors from *Beta Pavonis,* in lifeboat, approaching planet of unknown sun. No navigators among us. Destruction of ship occurred on twenty-third day of voyage from New Tasmania to Hunteria. I can give no further data. S O S. S O S."

"Do you expect a reply?" asked Gladen.

"I'd like to get one," said Kennedy, "but I'm afraid I don't expect one. Anyhow, the monitors will pick up this call—eventually. Too, once we've landed I'll run the transmitter once a day at the same time."

"So you intend to land?" asked Susan Weldon.

"What else is there? These boats are equipped to give occupants the maximum chance of survival. We have weapons. We have fishing gear. We have seeds, even. We have a well stocked medicine chest, and all the necessary books."

"Including one on obstetrics?" asked Gladen.

Kennedy felt himself blushing.

"Yes," he admitted.

"Never mind all this," blustered Fuller. "What do we do now?"

"Wait," said Kennedy. "Wait for all of two days—and perhaps a bit extra. It'll be safe enough for all of us to take our suits and helmets off now—although we'd better put them on again before we hit atmosphere."

"And if the atmosphere's poisonous," asked Tolliver, "shall we have enough fuel to take off again?"

"No," admitted Kennedy.

"Then there's not much sense in putting the suits back on," said Tolliver.

They waited.

They squabbled and bickered, and even the Grants were heard to snap at each other. They took turns at studying, through the telescope, the world towards which they were heading. There was water, and there was cloud, and there were polar icecaps. There were areas of brown, and areas of yellow, and areas of green. The certainty grew that this world would support life—their sort of life.

Then came the time when they were able to circle the world in a five hundred mile orbit. Kennedy was not willing to decide upon a landing place himself, so called upon the others to suggest and to advise. Some favoured desert, some the sea. In the end it was Gladen who said, "You're skipper of this craft, Kennedy. You make the decision—and if it's a wrong one you won't be the first captain who's been a bum guesser. And, right or wrong, I'm backing you."

"And I," said Susan Weldon.

"Don't hurry him into it," growled Major Fuller.

"I'm not," said Gladen. "But none of us here seems qualified to advise Mr. Kennedy—and he's the only one who's capable of landing this boat in one piece."

"I hope," said Tolliver.

"Shut up!" snarled his wife. "The situation's bad enough now without you making it worse with your wisecracks."

"I can hope, can't I?" he demanded plaintively.

"What hope is there?" burst out Mrs. Grant. "For any of us? It's all right for the rest of you—but I'm going to have my first child in that . . . wilderness! As for you," she screamed at her husband, "you said that everything would be all right—and now look what you've got me into!"

"In the Army," wheezed Fuller, "we . . ."

"*Damn* the Army," flared Grant.

"You see," said Gladen. "If we hang here in this orbit much longer there'll be murder done. There're one or two I shouldn't mind murdering myself."

"Not me, I hope, Stephen?" asked Susan Weldon.

"Yes—even you at times, my dear."

"Don't call me *dear!*" she snapped.

"Quiet!" shouted Kennedy. Then—"We're going down. I'm going to land at the edge of that green plain, by the river. If any of you have a better idea, let me hear it. But make it quick."

There was silence.

"All right. Fasten seat belts. Stand by for deceleration."

"Get it over with," said Gladen. "What I am doing? Don't disturb me."

Kennedy fired a tentative blast from the starboard steering jet, then another. The craft turned, slowly at first, then with increasing speed. Kennedy had to correct with a blast from the port jet.

The boat was proceeding stern first now, with her rockets pointed in the direction of her flight. A five seconds' blast from the main venturi killed her momentum. It was obvious, even without looking at the instruments, that she was falling.

Feeling increasingly confident, Kennedy turned the craft again. Rather incredulously he thought, *I'm good. I'm in the wrong branch of the Service. I should have been executive . . .*

"If you're coming in too fast," said Fuller, "you'll tear the wings off us."

"It's too late to worry about that now," replied Kennedy.

But I am so worrying, he thought. *I wish that that old fool would keep his mouth shut.*

Then there was sound—a thin, high keening, dropping slowly down the scale from the supersonic. There was heat, engendered by friction.

I should have made them put their spacesuits on, thought Kennedy. *They keep out the cold—they'd keep out the heat.*

Cautiously, he manipulated the controls. He felt the pressure against his back and seat as the ship lifted. The keening noise died away.

Down we go again, thought Kennedy. *I hope that this slows us down sufficiently . . .*

The fourth attempt did – and then Kennedy was concerned more with the location of his proposed landing site than with the actual handling of the boat. "They fly themselves," he had been told during his lifeboatman's course.

He found the sharp peak, thrusting up from the dense forest along the edge of the plain. He located, again, the broad, silver ribbon of the river. He put the craft into a tight spiral, using the peak as a beacon. He lost altitude fast, but speed not fast enough.

But he was impatient to get it all over and done with. He knew that he had one ace up his sleeve – the so-called "fool's rockets," the forward pointing tubes, each with its charge of solid propellant, that were supposed to be the last resort of the incompetent pilot.

They're there to be used, he thought.

The long grass was close now, ripples running over it under the wind. Kennedy skimmed the river, was barely conscious of the yellow beach that flashed by under him. He turned the ship, wrenching her around brutally so that she was heading up wind. He pressed the firing stud of the "fool's rockets."

He heard screams behind him. He heard something breaking. Then, as his safety belt snapped, he was thrown forward against the instrument panel. He did not feel the ship tilt and topple, he did not hear the horrid screech as the starboard stub wing was torn off; he was unconscious.

"He's coming round," he heard somebody say.

He opened his eyes.

He saw first of all a blue sky, with one or two small, fleecy clouds. Something large and black was flapping slowly across his field of vision, screaming discordantly as it flew. He smelt air that was *alive,* not the fetid, circulated and recirculated artificial atmosphere of the boat. He sniffed the tang of smouldering grass appreciatively.

"Wake up!" somebody was saying.

He shifted his eyes, saw the lean, intent face of Susan Weldon above him. Then Gladen moved to stand beside her.

"There's nothing broken," said the writer. "And, as far as I can gather from that book in the medicine chest, you haven't got concussion."

"Thanks," said Kennedy.

"Don't thank me–thank your thick skull."

"Help me up," said the assistant purser.

The man and the girl raised him to a sitting posture. He looked at the wreckage of his first and last command. Her vaned tail was in the air, her nose was in the pit that she had dug for herself. Around the rim of the pit the grass still smouldered. By the wreck sat the other passengers—Major Fuller, the Grants, the Tollivers. It seemed to Kennedy that they were looking at him with hostility.

"I'm afraid," said Kennedy, "that I made a mess of things."

"So what?" demanded Gladen. "We're all of us alive. Nobody's injured, even. Oh, I know that *they* think that you're the worst atmosphere pilot unhung—but none of them volunteered to do the job."

"I was saving fuel," said the assistant purser, "so that we could use the boat for exploring. But she'll never fly again."

"We stay in one place," said Gladen, "and that's all to the good. We keep the automatic beacon working—it seems to have survived the crash. We'll set up our camp here, and when the rescue ship homes on the beacon, its crew'll have no trouble finding us."

"It's as good a place as any," said Susan. "We have the river for fresh water and, perhaps, food. I've seen some things like crayfish. We have the forest for timber to build our houses—and it's a safe bet that some of the birds and animals there are edible . . ."

"Some of them might view us in the same light," said Gladen.

"Don't be such a damned pessimist, Stephen. Then, as I was saying, we can clear ourselves a few acres of grass and plant our seeds . . ."

"Quite the pioneer woman, aren't you, darling?" scoffed the writer. "This is a far cry from the Rag Trade!"

"Shut up!" she snapped.

"Yes, Gladen—shut up!" repeated Kennedy. "Miss Weldon was offering constructive suggestions—and all you could do was sneer."

"Were you ordering me around, young Kennedy? I'd like to point out that your pretty uniform ceased to have any significance once we touched—and a gentle touch it was, too—the surface of this planet."

Kennedy got to his feet, helped by the girl.

He said, disappointed that his voice was not as steady as it should have been, "I'd like to point out, Gladen, that there are still a lot of things to do that only I am qualified to handle. After they have been done I'll relinquish my command willingly. Until such time I'll stay in charge."

"All right. Take charge."

"Somebody has to," said Kennedy, glaring first at Gladen and then at the group loafing by the wrecked boat. He walked, stumbling slightly in the long grass, to the wreckage. "You," he said. "Fuller, Tolliver, Grant—get that fire out."

"Why?" asked Mrs. Tolliver. "It's not doing any harm."

"I wasn't addressing you, Madam. But you and Mrs. Grant can get back into the boat and pass out four of the shovels that you will find in the after compartment."

"Were you ordering *me?"* asked the big, untidy woman.

"Yes."

"In the Army, young man," began Fuller, "a junior officer . . ."

"This is not the Army, Major. In any case, as far as the Interstellar Commerce Commission is concerned, I'm the only officer present. And I want this fire out, before it spreads."

"We should have thought of it," admitted Tolliver.

"You should have—but you didn't."

"Into the boat, dear," said Tolliver to his wife.

"I'll not stand for this," she flared.

"You will!" he snarled—and there was such venom in his voice that she hoisted herself clumsily into the airlock door and vanished. Mrs. Grant followed her.

"Stay inside," Kennedy told them when they had passed out the shovels. "I'll want some more stores out shortly."

Working hard, if not very efficiently, they extinguished the blaze before it reached serious proportions. Kennedy climbed into the boat then, climbed aft to the storage compartment. He found the tents, and the cylinders of compressed carbon dioxide that would inflate them. He got out the solar power screens, and the batteries. When they were passed out to those outside, he set the women to work stripping the chairs inside the little rocket—their cushions were so designed as to serve as beds in the tents. While they were so employed, he broke out the armament.

There was a point fifty calibre Schuster automatic rifle, with a thousand rounds of ammunition. There were two point twenty Remingtons, with four thousand rounds. There were two twelve gauge Winchester repeating shotguns, with six thousand rounds. There were six of the deadly Minotti fifty shot automatics, whose makers said, with justification, that one of the tiny, exploding slivers properly placed could stop a charging bull elephant.

There were four long-bows, and a good supply of arrows. Kennedy hoped that the party would not be on this world long enough to have to fall back on the ancient, but still effective, weapons.

He belted on a holster with one of the automatics, hesitated between the Schuster and a Remington, finally slung the lighter weapon over his shoulder. The others, with the exception of Gladen, looked at him askance when he emerged from the ship. Gladen grinned.

"So you're going to enforce your authority by force of arms," he remarked.

Kennedy kept his temper.

"There are five more pistols inside, by the airlock door. If any of you can use them, you're welcome to belt them on. There's a point fifty rifle, and another point twenty, and two shotguns. These weapons are here for two reasons—for our protection and to provide game for the pot. I think that at least one of us—until we're sure that there are no dangers here—should go armed all the time."

"I wish that I had your imagination," said Gladen, half seriously.

"It's not imagination. It's just knowing all the things could possibly go wrong, and then doing one's best to cope with them. Meanwhile—do any of you know how to get these tents up?"

Nobody did.

Kennedy took off his weapons, handed them to Fuller.

"You're sentry," he said.

"When I was in the Army, young man . . ."

". . . Majors never did sentry duty. But even Majors must know something about firearms. Just be careful about opening fire—there's always the chance that you might antagonize some local intelligent life form."

"If any," said Gladen.

"Oh, shut up, Gladen. Lend a hand with this, will you?"

There were four tents, each of them neatly packaged. Kennedy broke the fastenings on the first one, pulled out the valve. He connected it to the cylinder of carbon dioxide, gave the wheel a quarter turn. The tent filled slowly, swelling and rustling. When it was fully expanded it was a gleaming, plastic igloo, a fifteen foot diameter hemisphere. There were translucent panels in its sides to admit the passage of daylight, and there were even opaque curtains inside that could be let down to cover these. Flared tubes—each of which could be sealed if necessary—through the double skin allowed for ventilation.

Kennedy checked the netting and the guy ropes to see that there was no chafe, then drove home the pegs in a circle around the tent, made all secure.

He left the Grants, the Tollivers and Susan Weldon to set up the other tents; he, aided by Gladen, busied himself with the solar power screen. This was not arduous work—the only part of the job that made any real demands upon his energy was the adjustment of it so that it would drag the maximum power output from the westering sun. Once this was done the efficient, almost intelligent little azimuth motor would keep the screen on the most advantageous bearing until sunset. By that time, Kennedy hoped, there would be enough power stored in the batteries to suffice for cooking of the evening meal and for lights during the hours of darkness. The lifeboat's storage cells could have been used for both purposes—but the spaceman wanted to be self sufficient as soon as possible.

Somebody was calling, "Smoko! Smoko!"

He looked up from the screen controls, saw that it was Susan Weldon. She was standing in the doorway of the first erected tent. She was rattling a spoon inside a cup.

"I boiled the kettle," she called, "and made tea for us all! This is our house warming!"

"Tea!" grimaced Gladen. "Surely there's something better, Kennedy."

"There is," said the assistant purser. "It's in the medicine chest. And it's staying there."

Kennedy walked to the tent.

"What water did you use, Miss Weldon?"

"The water from the ship's tank, of course."

"Just as well. We still have to test the river water. Boiling would kill any micro-organisms, but there may be mineral poisons."

"How will you test it?" asked Gladen.

"There's a kit for doing so in the medicine chest. But I could do with a good cup of tea, and I'm having it. Major Fuller—that will do the sentry duty for the time being. Tea break!"

It was comfortable inside the tent—but, of course, the tent had been designed for comfort as well as for its other qualities. The scene, thought Kennedy, was absurdly domesticated—the seven people sitting on their cushions around the spread cloth, the steaming teapot and hot water jug, the cups, the saucers, the sugar bowl, the jug of evaporated milk. On no world, he thought, have we yet found anything to take the place of tea. I hope that we find some herb here that will be a good substitute . . .

"What now, Kennedy?" asked Fuller.

"We'll get our camp set up for the night. We'll work out a watch list. We'll get as good a night's sleep as possible, so that we're ready for some exploring tomorrow."

"A watch list . . ." said Mrs. Grant. "You really think that there might be dangerous animals here?"

"Or savages," said Gladen, grinning again.

"Or savages," agreed Kennedy. "Until we know more, we have to be prepared for *anything.*"

"Are *we*—the women, I mean—among the watchkeepers?" asked Susan Weldon. "I can use a Minotti."

"No," replied Kennedy definitely.

"What old-fashioned ideas you have," remarked the writer.

"I'm keeping watch with Bill, anyhow," said Mrs. Grant defiantly.

"Let her," said Gladen. "Two pairs of eyes are better than one. Will you keep watch with me, Susan?"

"I will *not,*" she said.

"We'll make out the roster later,"

said Kennedy briskly. "The next item on the agenda is accommodation. We have two married couples, one unmarried woman, three unmarried men. We have four tents. You, Mr. and Mrs. Tolliver, take one of them. You, Mr. and Mrs. Grant, take one of the others. You, Miss Weldon, will have a tent to yourself. Major Fuller, Mr. Gladen and myself will share the fourth one. It's lucky that we have the equipment for over seven times our number of people."

"It could be a pity," said Gladen. "Anyhow—if you're lonely, Susan, I've no doubt that friend Kennedy, here, could put us through a form of marriage sufficiently legal to stick."

"I shall be quite happy by myself," said the girl—and Kennedy was relieved to hear her say it. He was, somehow, disappointed when she added, "I always have been."

"The most pressing item on the agenda now," said Kennedy, "is digging the trench and rigging the screens for the latrine."

"The man has no romance in his soul," said Gladden.

Kennedy had the fourth spell of duty—2400 hours to 0200 hours. All watches owned by the party had been set at 1800 hours at sunset—the lifeboat's chronometer, of course, had not been tampered with; the automatic distress signal would be sent out at six hourly intervals by ship's time, Greenwich Mean Time.

Kennedy wondered, when Gladen called him, if this planet did, in fact, have a period of roughly twenty-four hours axial rotation. It was one of the things that he could have checked during their approach to it from space—if he had known enough.

He got dressed by the dim light of the battery-powered lamp, moving carefully so as not to disturb Fuller—although if the fat Major were a light sleeper his own snoring must surely have awakened him. He belted on the pistol. When he was outside the tent Gladen handed him one of the point twenty rifles.

"The watch is yours," said Gladen.

"I wonder if it *is* midnight," said Kennedy. "There's a sort of midnightish feel in the air . . ." He looked up at the sky, wishing that he knew enough astronomy to hazard a guess as to the location of this planet. There was a Milky Way—but it was subtly different from the Milky Way as seen from Earth. There was a sprawling constellation that could have been a distorted Orion, and another one that wound sinuously across the black sky like a huge serpent, with a blazing star cluster at its head. There was no moon—but that he had already known.

"Anything to report?" he asked.

"No. I walked over to the edge of the forest, but I heard no noises indicative of large animals. Then I stood for a while by the river—there were quite a few splashes, but small ones. We must break out the fishing gear tomorrow."

"You should have stayed by the camp," said Kennedy.

"I'm old enough," replied Gladen, "to use my own discretion—and I used it. Goodnight to you."

"I wish that you weren't such a cantankerous bastard at times," said the assistant purser.

"You know," said the writer—and Kennedy could see his teeth gleaming in the near darkness—"there're times when I wish the same myself. Goodnight again."

"Where are you going? That's Miss Weldon's tent."

"Don't be such an innocent," replied Gladen.

Kennedy, feeling more than a little sick, walked away from the tents. Something made him turn. The light in the girl's tent snapped on, at full brilliance. Gladen—a black silhouette—was still in the doorway. Kennedy saw him turn abruptly, walk back to the tent he shared with Fuller and Kennedy. He was whistling. The assistant purser recognized the tune—it was one of the Twentieth Century songs that had, of late, been revived. It was *Lay That Pistol Down, Babe* . . .

I wonder . . . thought Kennedy. I wonder . . . After all, if we're to be on this world for any length of time . . .

Should I walk up and down? he asked himself abruptly. Or should I stay still? If I walk I make a noise, and let anything creeping up on the camp know where I am. If I stand still—well, a wild animal would hear me breathing, or scent me, so what's the odds? I should have rigged floodlights—and made a glare that would have attracted savages (if there are any) from miles around. The others have the best of it—they sit back and criticize, but none of them's willing to take over command . . .

Anyhow, if we are on this world for any length of time . . . Gladen's her type really, that's the trouble . . .

Suddenly he snapped out of his revery, whipped the pistol from its holster with his right hand, switched on the torch that he carried in the other.

"Put that light out," said Susan Weldon rather crossly. "Do you want to blind me?"

"I thought you were sleeping," he said foolishly.

"Sleeping, the man says. Sleeping—with wolves pawing at the door of my tent."

"Only one wolf. I saw him slinking away with his tail between his legs."

"Not quite," she said. "I'll say this for Stephen—he took it all in good part. After all—he didn't want me quite badly enough to have a shooting match with me."

"Just as well," said Kennedy. "It'd have been a nuisance if the tent had got punctured."

"I notice that you weren't worried about either Stephen or myself getting punctured," she said tartly.

"The tent is stores," he pointed out. "You and Stephen are only passengers."

"I see," she said. "I'm pleased to learn that you do regard me as a human being. I was beginning to think that you were regarding me as just an item on the store list, or something."

"I've always thought rather highly of you," he said.

"Too highly, perhaps. Will it be all right to smoke?"

He considered the matter. He said at last. "I have noticed a few things like fireflies flitting around, and some of them have a ruddy light. Our cigarettes could be mistaken for fireflies by any potential enemy . . ."

"That's as good an excuse for a smoke as any," she said.

He pulled the packet of cigarettes out of the breast pocket of his shirt, found the filter ends by touch, put them in his mouth. He inhaled sharply. He handed one of the little cylinders to the girl. She did not draw her hand back when his touched it.

He said, "We have to remember that our supplies are not unlimited."

"And that the duration of our stay here might well be," she added.

The ruddy illumination of the cigarette showed him her face—thin, serious, the eyes seeming larger and darker than they were in actuality, the mouth wide, with a potentiality of generosity.

"That's a fact that we have to face," he said.

"That's a fact that I am facing. I'm a young woman and, they tell me, attractive. I've never had much time for men—there's always been my career. But I can't see much scope for my talents on this planet. So . . ."

"So," he asked, "what?"

"So I have to think of somebody permanent. Somebody who'll be my protector, and the father of my brats. And there's not much choice. Even if Grant and Tolliver were free I'd never consider either of them—I've never fancied suburbia. Fuller's out. It's between you and Stephen.

"Oh, I like Stephen. At times he's fun. But there's that laziness of his, and his failure to take the right things—by which I don't mean what the Tollivers and the Grants consider the right things—seriously. He could be a leader—but he'll never take the responsibility. He's a born barracker."

"So I'm elected," said Kennedy quietly.

"So you're not elected. Not yet. After all, Ralph, there's no mad rush. I like you—but whether or not I like you enough to live with you is another matter."

"I rather hope . . ." began Kennedy. "Oh, damn it. How shall I put it? I hope that you do make the decision in my favor."

"I rather hope," she said, "that I do."

She threw her cigarette away, then reached up and plucked his from his mouth. She took his face between her hands, raised her lips to his. It was a brief kiss—yet enough to stir desire. She broke away from him.

"Goodnight," she said. "And I mean goodnight."

"I'll be looking forward to saying goodmorning," he replied.

"By the morning," she laughed, "I might have decided in favor of polyandry."

"I make the laws here," he reminded her.

"Then you'd better take a dim view of the sentries philandering whilst on duty. Goodnight again."

She vanished into her tent.

Kennedy was amazed when he looked at the luminous figures on the dial of his watch and saw that his spell of duty was up. He walked to the Grants' tent, scratched on the plastic screen that had been let down to cover the doorway. There was no answer. He lifted the screen then, went inside.

"Grant," he called softly. "Grant!"

He called again, louder.

There was a flurry of motion on the makeshift bed. Kennedy glimpsed pale limbs and breasts, dimly luminous in the starlight. He envied Grant, and wished that his own future marital state were more certain. He backed out of the tent.

After a few minutes Grant and his wife joined him. Kennedy handed over the watch, making sure that the man and the woman were both armed and knew how to handle their weapons.

"And pass on to Fuller," he said, "and tell him to pass it on to Gladen, that I want the *exact* time of sunrise noted. We must get some idea of how time runs on this planet."

"I don't think that time's all that important," murmured Mrs. Grant.

"I do," said Kennedy, with unnecessary sharpness.

"There's no need to talk to Rose like that!" snapped Grant.

"Sorry," said Kennedy insincerely.

He walked to the tent, lifted the flap, went inside. Fuller was still snoring. Gladen was asleep—but restless in his slumber, twisting and muttering.

"Susan," Kennedy heard him mumble. "Susan, please . . ."

What with the pair of them, thought Kennedy, I shall be lucky to get any sleep at all. I wonder if Susan would let me in to her tent? But I forgot. I must set the good example. I'm the Captain—Acting, Temporary, Unpaid . . .

He undressed, not bothering overduly with quietness. He got under his own blankets. In spite of Fuller's snores, of Gladen's mutterings, he dropped immediately into unconsciousness . . .

. . . and awoke with the sound of the scream still ringing in his ears.

Susan, he thought. If that swine Gladen . . .

But it was Gladen who had snapped on the light, who was stepping into his shorts and buckling on his pistol belt. Kennedy didn't bother to dress—just grabbed his pistol and a torch and ran outside. Fuller was still snoring.

The beam of another torch hit him in the face, travelled down his body.

"Ralph! What are you doing?"

"Thank God," he said. "Thank God that it wasn't you!"

"That it wasn't me who *what?*" she asked.

"Screamed. But what's happened?"

"Nothing," she said. "Well—almost nothing. The pair of lovebirds sat down just outside my tent and started chirruping away to each other, and I was just about to get up to tell them to pitch woo somewhere else when I heard her say, 'Oh, isn't he *cute!*' He said, 'He's like those animals we saw in Australia, last time we were on Earth . . . What did they call them? Koala bears, wasn't it? Here—Teddy, Teddy, Teddy!' And *she* called, 'Teddy, Teddy, Teddy!' And then she screamed."

"You're not being paid ten cents a word for this," said Gladen. "Come to the point, darling, before our nudist friend freezes to death."

"All right. As far as I can gather, this Teddy Bear of hers made a sudden, vicious and unprovoked attack and bit her on the neck. It's no more than a scratch. She's back in her tent now, and old Mother Tolliver is flapping around her like a hen with only one chick—and that one at death's store. I was coming to call you."

"I'd better see her," said Kennedy.

"You'd better get dressed first," Gladen told him. "Poor Rosie's had enough shocks for one night."

"While I'm getting dressed," said Kennedy, "slip into the boat and go to the medicine chest. Bring out one of the tubes labelled *All-Purpose Antibiotic*. The bite may be as trivial as Susan says—but it may be badly infected."

"It is extremely unlikely that the micro-organisms of any one planet will be able to harm any alien species," said Gladen.

"I know—but whoever made the regulations concerning how medicine chests should be stocked didn't make 'em for fun. Get cracking!"

"Ay, ay, *sir,*" said Gladen.

Susan followed him into the tent, talked to him while he dressed.

"Could it be serious?" she asked. "After all—there *are* such things as poisonous snakes . . ."

"Oddly enough," he said, "the ability to kill by poison seems to be confined entirely to reptiles and insects. I see no reason to assume that this planet is any exception to the general rule."

"There's one exception on Earth," she said. "A mammal, and it lives in the same country as the Koala bears that the Grants were yapping about. The platypus."

"It's got a spur, if I remember rightly," admitted Kennedy. "But it doesn't bite its victims. Let's go."

"What about *him?*" asked Susan, pointing one slim foot in the direction of the sleeping Fuller.

"Let him sleep on."

The Grants' tent was commodious enough—but now it seemed crowded, largely because of Mrs. Tolliver. She was one of those women always determined to make the most of any minor household calamity, one of those to whom there is almost no dividing line between a cut finger and decapitation. Grant was trying to get his well meaning visitors away.

"There's no danger," he kept saying. "There's absolutely no danger. If there was any poison in the wound there's none now—I sucked it out . . ."

Kennedy pushed his way past the Tollivers.

"Let me see," he said.

"If you *must,*" growled Grant ungraciously.

The assistant purser knelt down beside the girl. She was half sitting, half lying on the bed, her back propped with extra cushions. She was pale, but seemed to be in no pain.

"Do you mind if I look?" asked Kennedy.

"It's only a scratch," she said.

The wound, indeed, was little more than a scratch, no more than a faint red line marring the smooth whiteness of her neck. There were no signs of either swelling or inflammation—but it was early yet for either to put in appearance.

Gladen knelt beside Kennedy.

"Here's that goo of yours," he said, handing Kennedy the tube.

"Thanks. Now, Mrs. Grant, I'm afraid that this is going to sting a little—but I can guarantee that it's sudden death to any and every micro-organism known to medical science . . ."

"It *does* sting," said Mrs. Grant in a tone of hurt bewilderment.

"I suppose you know what you're doing," said Grant.

"Poor dear," said Mrs. Tolliver. "Warm water was all it needed."

"You stay here, with your wife," said Kennedy to Grant. "The rest of you—and that means you, too, Mrs. Tolliver—get torches. We'll see if we can find the little brute that bit Mrs. Grant. It may be lurking around still."

They found the little brute without much trouble. It was about five yards from Susan Weldon's tent. It was dead—killed, thought Kennedy, by the blow that Grant had dealt it when it attacked his wife.

It was as much like a Koala bear

as anything, but its fur was yellow and it had a bushy tail. It could not have died at once, thought Kennedy; the front of its body, from the mouth downwards, was wet and bedraggled. It must have sat there in the grass, choking and strangling, coughing its life out.

Now I'm getting sentimental about it, he thought.

He asked Gladen to hold the torch while he examined the creature's open mouth. It had teeth—small ones. There were no signs of poison fangs.

"She must have been petting it," he said. "She must have touched it in a tender place, and it went for her, the same as a cat or dog will." He looked at his watch. "You might as well take over until four, Tolliver. Call Fuller then. And don't forget about the time of sunrise, if the sun comes up while you're on."

He picked up the animal by the tail.

"A fur coat for me?" asked Susan.

"Maybe. One day—if we can trap enough of these. I just want to keep it so I can have a better look at it in daylight."

Daylight came, and found a party of humans reluctant to arise to greet the dawn. Kennedy was as reluctant as any of them—but dared not show it. He almost drove the men to the part of the river that he had decided would be their bathing place. Susan, he was pleased to see, did the same regarding the women, not forgetting to complain that the ladies' bath was downstream from the men's.

Then there was breakfast, which they enjoyed in the open air. The powdered egg made a palatable enough omelette and the tea, brewed over an open fire instead of being made in a conventional pot, was good. Kennedy watched Rose Grant carefully, was pleased to see that she ate with a good appetite. The mark on her neck had almost vanished.

"What now?" asked Gladen, enjoying his after-breakfast cigarette.

"The camp chores we leave to the women," said Kennedy. "You, Major Fuller and Mr. Tolliver, will be camp guards. Gladen, Grant and myself will take a little walk into the forest."

"I think I should stay with Rose," said Grant.

"Mr. Grant," said Susan, "doubtless both Mr. Kennedy and Mr. Gladen would prefer to stay here with me—but they recognize that there's important work to be done."

"Talking of work," said Gladen, "I could be making a start on my next novel."

"Don't be silly, Stephen. You and Ralph are going out like two Stone Age types, to return loaded with meat to fill our bellies and furs to cover our nakedness. Talking of furs—where's our little friend of last night, Ralph?"

"In the tent still. I'll bring him out."

He did so.

"I still think he looks cute," said Rose Grant. "I still think that you shouldn't have hit him so hard, Bill."

"I wish that I'd hit him harder," growled Grant.

"Well," said Kennedy. "We're none of us biologists, unluckily. I suggest that you, Major, give this unfortunate animal a burial with full military honors. And I suggest, too, that if you see any more of 'em lurking around you open fire at once."

"I'll have my fur coat yet," said Susan. Then—"Hey! What about the washing up?"

"The Stone Age wife's privilege," said Gladen. "Where's Grant vanished to?"

"They're saying goodbye in their tent," said Kennedy.

"The *dears,*" gushed Mrs. Tolliver.

"Of course, they haven't been married long," said her husband.

"Grant!" shouted Kennedy. "Grant!"

"All right, I'm coming. What's the rush?"

"We'll try to be back at twelve hundred hours," said Kennedy to Fuller. "That is, according to the time that our watches are set at now. If anything happens—*if* anything happens—loose off a shotgun; they make the biggest bang. We'll do the same. But if *we* do it, don't come a-running unless you're sure that the women are safe."

"They'll be safe with the *Army,*" said Fuller.

"This is the Merchant Navy," said Kennedy foolishly.

"Well I know it," replied the Major.

"Look here, Fuller," said the assistant purser, "if you want to take charge—take charge. I'm getting tired of all this barracking."

"It's your job," said Fuller.

"Oh, all right. Where's Grant? Everybody got everything — weapons, knives, machete, compass? Then let's go."

The three men walked along the river bank, towards the forest.

"There's no planet I've seen," said Gladen, "as much like Earth as this one. This grass that we're walking over, for example. Those reeds . . ."

Grant pulled himself out of his sulking fit.

"Given almost identical conditions — mass, atmospheric content and density, humidity, temperature range and all the rest of it—evolution is bound to run on similar lines."

"Not necessarily," said Gladen. "Were you ever on Altair IV? It has all the conditions for Earth-type life forms—but every living thing has its chemistry based on silica."

"For all we know," contributed Kennedy, "the same might be true here, and everything might be quite inedible."

"I don't think so," said Gladen. "The plants haven't that peculiar crystalline shine." He stopped, bent down, plucked a blade of grass, put it to his mouth, nibbled it. "I've never tasted better!"

"Be careful!" snapped Kennedy. "That stuff may be a deadly poison!"

"And so what? Somebody has to be the guinea pig—and it might as well be me. I would suggest somebody recommend that lifeboats carry white mice or some similar animal—they'd be useful for the testing of local foodstuffs. H'm. Those berries look interesting."

"Don't be a damned fool!" said Kennedy.

"'What care I how fair she be,/ If she be not fair to me . . .'" replied the writer.

"What are you yapping about?" asked Grant.

"None of your business—yet."

"And just what do you mean by that, Gladen? Are you insinuating that because the Weldon woman kicked you out of her tent last night you're thinking of making a pass at Rose? How big a fool can you be? She'd never look at another man but me."

"'Methinks the gentleman doth protest too much,'" replied the writer. "All right, Grant, don't go flying off the handle. I'll quote from the works of my old cobber Bill Shakespeare as much as I please." He turned to Kennedy. "Has the sobering thought ever crossed your mind that if we *do* have to build a new civilization here, I shall be the sole repository of Earth's greatest literature? I think you'd better organize a supply of flat slabs of granite for me, and a hammer and chisel."

"Oh, shut up!" snarled Grant.

A flight of birds flapped over, low, uttering discordant cries. Kennedy, who was carrying the shotgun, raised it—then let the muzzle of the weapon drop.

"What's wrong?" asked Gladen. "Coming over all humanitarian? Going to start a local branch of the Anti-Blood Sports League?"

Kennedy blushed.

"No. I remembered that we agreed that a shot was to be the signal that there was something amiss. If I fired—I'd alarm them back at the camp."

"I'd like to see fat Fuller charging out like the legendary U. S. Marines in full cry," commented Gladen. "All the same, young Kennedy, that was a rather backhanded system of signals you arranged."

"I know. Why didn't somebody point it out at the time?"

"Grant was too busy—and my mind was on other things. Fuller and Tolliver don't count. Or can't count. I often wonder which of the two is the dimmer."

"I suppose that if I weren't here," said Grant, "you'd be discussing me."

"Of course, dearie. There's nothing that Ralph and I like more than an all-girls-together session over the tea cups, with our hair down and our feet up. We have *so* much in common, haven't we, Ralph?"

"I've more in common with Grant at the moment," snapped Kennedy. "You may be enjoying this cats' corner, but I'm not. And we're supposed to be exploring, not gossiping."

"Yessir. Ay, ay, sir. Can I come back next trip, sir?"

"All right," laughed Kennedy. "You win. But let's pay a little more attention to the matter in hand."

"There's something in the grass," said Grant. "An animal . . ."

"A bird," corrected Gladen.

"It's dead," added Kennedy. He wrinkled his nose. "It's very dead."

"We can look at it, anyhow," said Gladen.

"As long as we don't touch it. The thing's probably crawling with bacteria."

"Of all shapes, colours and sizes—not to mention the odd virus or two. Ugly looking brute, isn't it? Like an Earthly vulture—only more so. I'm sorry that I have to keep on comparing things with their Terran counterparts—but, after all, I was brought up there."

"Local boy makes good," sneered Grant.

"Precisely. At least I'm not living on the money my father made as a New Morocco white slave trader."

"He was a theatrical agent," said Grant.

"Let's look at this bloody bird!" shouted Kennedy.

They looked at the bird. At first it seemed just a bird—large, limp, bedraggled. It was Kennedy who found the long stick and turned it over; who, by dint of poking and prodding, managed to stretch the wings to their full, four foot spread. It was then that they saw the perfectly formed claw on each wing tip.

"This must be a primitive world," said Kennedy slowly. "There may be dinosaurs—or things like 'em—in the forest."

"Could be," murmured Gladen. "Could be—but I don't think so. That mammal that Grant killed last night didn't seem any more primitive than, say, an Earthly dog or cat."

"But these claws . . ."

"What about them? Oh, I know that on most planets with anything approximating to Earth-type fauna, Mother Nature, in her alleged wisdom, has allowed the wing tip claws to vanish. Once the birds could fly properly, once they had no need to make wild grabs for branches when they stalled, the claws were of no further use. But—any bird, no matter how well it flies, could always use an extra set of claws. Our friend here could handle things without having to stand on one leg to do it. It's the same with tails. We should never have been allowed to lose ours when we came down from the trees. A prehensile tail would be of great value to civilized man."

"Oh, shut up!" snarled Grant.

Gladen and Kennedy glared at him.

It was Kennedy who said, "What's wrong, Grant? You don't look well."

"I don't feel well. This headache. You two carry on—I'll get back to the camp."

"You might pass out on the way," said Kennedy. "We'll come with you."

In spite of Grant's indisposition they made the journey back in shorter time than it had taken them to come as far as they had done. As they approached the tents, the wrecked lifeboat, they saw only one figure, pacing slowly back and forth.

"It's Tolliver," decided Kennedy. "The women must be in the boat getting a meal together. Fuller, if I know him, is snatching a nap. He'll be quite pained when we catch him out."

"Or he's in the galley," said Gladen, "helping with lunch and having an occasional nibble of what's going to keep his strength up. 'In the Army,' he mimicked, 'we always built up a reserve of strength against any contingency.'"

"It's time we started living off the country," said Kennedy.

"Stop worrying, Ralph."

"You're back early," called Tolliver. He walked to meet them. "I took the fishing tackle to the river. I found some worms to use as bait. I caught three fine seven pounders—they look as near to trout as to be their twin brothers."

"Where's Rose?" demanded Grant. "Tell her that I'm back and that I'm going to lie down."

"She's in your tent, I think. She wasn't feeling too good herself."

"I'll get you something from the medicine chest," said Kennedy to Grant.

He saw that the young man was staggering. He and Gladen walked with him to the tent.

The flap was down. It was secured from the inside.

"Rose!" shouted Grant. "Open up! It's me!"

"She must be asleep," said Gladen.

"Rose! Open this damned flap!"

Grant tore himself from the supporting arms of Kennedy and Gladen. His strong fingers caught a fold in the material of the flap, ripped viciously. Grant made a noise that was half way between a snarl and a scream, that was like nothing human. He charged into the semi-darkness. Kennedy followed—and tripped and fell headlong. Gladen stumbled over Kennedy's body. There was the staccato rattle of a Minetti automatic, and another scream from Grant.

Kennedy scrambled to his feet, pulled his own pistol from its holster. He looked in horror at the tableau—at Grant, sprawled on the floor, the wound in his belly spilling blood and shredded intestines, at Rose Grant, half naked, sprawled obscenely across the bed, one side of her head blown off, at the fat Major, whose condition of undress would in other circumstances have been ludicrous, standing there with the still smoking automatic in his hand.

"I didn't mean to kill her," he was babbling. "But I had to shoot *him* in self defense!"

"Drop the gun," ordered Kennedy. Then, to Gladen, "Stand by the door and keep the women and Tolliver out—they must have heard the shooting."

He waited until Fuller had dropped his pistol, then stooped and picked up the pair of shorts that he had tripped over in the doorway, threw them to the fat man.

"You'd better put these on," he said. "If you're going to die—and I'm the law here—you'd better do it with some semblance of dignity."

Fuller dressed. With the resumption of his clothing something of his old manner came back.

"Let me explain, young man," he began.

"An explanation is just what I do want. If Grant had killed you it would have been justifiable homicide. But you killed Grant—*and* his wife."

"Susan," Gladen was saying at the doorway, "there's nothing you can do. Go away, please—and take Mr. and Mrs. Tolliver with you. We'll tell you all about it later."

"He came at me like a wild beast," cried Fuller. "He . . . He attacked me with his teeth. Look!" His hand went up to the side of his neck, came away crimson. "I think that you should get this wound dressed before you do anything else."

"It can wait," said Kennedy. "I still want to know what happened."

"I told you. He came at us like a wild beast. Luckily my belt was by the bed. In the Army we were taught never to leave our weapons out of reach. My first shot wasn't enough. We struggled. One of the shots must have hit Rose."

"That much is obvious. *But what happened?*"

"It wasn't my fault, Kennedy. In the Army we were taught to respect another fellow's wife. But she made a play for me all the morning. And . . . Well, damn it all, Kennedy, I'm still a young man, and a slice from a cut cake is never missed. And I knew that there was plenty of time before you were due back. If I'd known that Grant would come sneaking back hours before the time. . ."

"I think he's right," said Gladen. "It's pretty obvious that it wasn't rape."

"It's still murder," said Kennedy.

"No, I don't think so. It was self defense. Damn it all, man—haven't you ever been caught with your pants down by an irate husband?"

"No," said Kennedy.

"Then you've been lucky."

"I haven't played around with married women, Gladen."

"That's your misfortune. Let me tell you, anyhow, that if I'd been in Fuller's shoes—or out of his trousers—and I'd seen Grant coming for me with that expression on his face, I'd have grabbed the first weapon handy and let fly. This is my advice, Kennedy. Don't do anything rash. Don't add murder to murder. Let the law deal with Fuller such time as we're picked up."

"I suppose you're right," admitted Kennedy at last.

"Of course I'm right."

"Very well." He turned to Fuller. "Get this shambles cleared up. I suppose that we'll have to let the women in to lay out the corpses..."

"Mrs. Tolliver'll never forgive you if you don't," said Gladen.

Kennedy glared at him.

"Get this shambles cleared up, Fuller. Gladen and I will carry the bodies to another tent."

Kennedy read the solemn words over the grave—then, aided by Gladen and Tolliver, he shovelled the earth into the pit. Fuller was there, but standing well back and to one side. Susan and Mrs. Tolliver were there, and Mrs. Tolliver's somehow indecent sobbing contrasted ill with the younger woman's dry-eyed, dignified yet real sorrow.

It was after dark when they sat down to their evening meal, which was served in Susan's tent. There had been considerable discussion about whether or not Fuller was to be allowed to eat with them. Kennedy was against it—but, he was rather surprised to discover, he was a minority of one. And he admitted to himself that his reasons for wishing to make a pariah of the unfortunate Fuller were emotional rather than intellectual.

It didn't really matter, anyhow, because Fuller died that night.

He went mad before he died. It started when he choked and spluttered over his tea and threw the cup from him. Tolliver, who was spattered by the hot liquid, said something in protest—and then went down under the Major's ferocious attack.

Tolliver would have died then, too, had it not been for the quickness of his wife. Moving with a speed incredible in one so gross she picked up a knife, flung herself on top of the struggling men and stabbed. She went on stabbing, long after the need to do so had passed. Kennedy and Gladen had to exert all of their strength to pull her off Fuller's body.

Tolliver got unsteadily to his feet. His face was bloody—but most of it was Fuller's blood. He said,

"I . . . I think I'm going to be sick . . ."

Mrs. Tolliver turned on Kennedy, waving the knife.

"That . . . *beast!*" she screamed. "Poor Mr. Grant, and that poor little wife of his, and now poor George! And you're supposed to be protecting us!"

"He must have been mad," said Kennedy inadequately.

"Of course he was mad. A mad dog—that's all that he was. And you, you . . . *puppy,* let him sit down at table with us."

"*We* decided not to treat him as a criminal," said Susan Weldon coldly. "All of us. And I seem to remember your saying, at the time, that Mrs. Grant deserved all she got."

Mrs. Tolliver glared at her, then turned to her husband.

"Come with me, George," she said. "I'll get you cleaned up."

The big woman and the little man left the tent.

"Well?" asked Gladen, of nobody in particular.

"He was mad," said Kennedy. "I saw his face as he attacked little Tolliver. He was quite mad."

"Why?" asked Gladen.

"You tell me," said Kennedy. "You're the writer around here. You know what makes people tick."

Gladen said, "Fuller—for all his military rank—was a peaceful, law-abiding citizen. Anybody further removed from the brutal and licentious soldiery of fiction it would be hard to imagine. I well believe that it was Mrs. Grant who seduced him, and not the other way round. So—this peaceful, law-abiding citizen commits murder. Oh, it might have been in self defense, but it was not in very creditable circumstances. He brooded, as you or I might have brooded—*you* would—and it drove him round the bend."

"That's the way I'll write it up in the Log," said Kennedy. "Meanwhile—we'd better have another funeral. I don't suppose that the Tollivers will want to be among the mourners."

They got the shovels out again. Working by the light of two of the battery-powered lanterns they dug another grave, all of twenty feet from the grave occupied by the Grants. Kennedy was reading the Burial Service when the Tollivers returned from the river. Mrs. Tolliver interrupted him.

"Never mind that," she said roughly. "You'd better do something about George's face. That man Fuller *bit* him."

Gladen inspected the wound.

"It's hardly a scratch," he said.

"Even so, we'd better use the antibiotic," said Kennedy. "Carry on filling the grave, Gladen—I'll dress Mr. Tolliver's wound now. Then we'll meet in our tent for a conference."

When the minor wound had been dressed, when everybody was

seated in the tent, Kennedy said, "I may be wrong. I hope I am. But it seems to me that there's something in the very air of this place that breeds murder. That's the danger here—nothing from outside, but only ourselves."

"And what are you doing about it?" asked Gladen.

"This is my idea. From now on we drop all ideas of modesty. From now on we all sleep in the one tent, so that if any one of us be seized by homicidal mania the others will be on hand to drag him off his victim."

"No," said Gladen. "That'd make things worse, I think. If we're all cooped up in the same tent, then tempers are going to become even more frayed than they are already. We shall increase the risk of murder, not lessen it. What I propose is this—that the two women sleep in the lifeboat—they should be safe enough behind the airlock doors. The three of us will carry on as before, splitting the night into watches."

"That's all very well," objected Kennedy, "but if any of us should go the same way as Grant or Fuller . . ."

"What reason is there that any of us should?" asked the writer. "Grant saw something that made him see red, that stripped the veneer of civilization from him in one microsecond. Fuller reacted as primitive man would have reacted —faced with a danger from which he could not run, he fought back. Successfully. Then remorse set in, and he wasn't tough enough to take it. Of course, I grant that I might have grounds for trying to murder *you,* Kennedy . . ."

"That was not funny," said Susan Weldon.

"It wasn't meant to be. But you needn't worry, my dear. I'm too civilized to go around murdering people."

"That's one of the things that's wrong with you," she said.

"You want it all ways, don't you?" he rebuked her. "Civilized when you want me civilized, uncivilized when you don't."

"Shut up, Stephen," she snapped.

"That'll be all from both of you," said Kennedy. "We'll turn to right away to get the inside of the boat fixed up as a bedroom for the ladies, and when that's finished we'll set our watches."

"I don't want to sleep in the boat," said Mrs. Tolliver.

"It will be the safest place," said Kennedy.

At last he, Tolliver, Gladen and Susan Weldon were able to convince her that this was so.

Gladen called Kennedy when it was time for his spell of duty.

He waited until the assistant purser was well out of earshot from the tent, in which Tolliver was still sleeping, before he started to talk.

"I hope," he said, "that you don't have such a wearing time as I did."

"What's wrong?"

"What's wrong? you ask. There am I, walking up and down, minding my own business, when suddenly a pair of female arms are flung around my neck and a big, wet mouth is planted on mine. Oh, no, you needn't worry. It wasn't our Susan. I shouldn't have minded *that.*"

"Not Mrs. Tolliver?" asked Kennedy.

"Yes, Mrs. Tolliver. Old Ma Tolliver in person. She slobbered all over me, and told me that her dear George had never been able to give her a child, and that it was up to us to become the Adam and Eve of this new world. I declined the honor as politely as I could—which wasn't very. Then I looked at my watch and saw that it was time to call you—and that gave me a good excuse to break the clinch."

"Where is she now?"

"I don't know. Prowling around, I suppose. *You'd* better watch out."

"She doesn't like me," said Kennedy thankfully.

"I didn't think that she liked me," replied the other. "But love's a wonderful thing . . ."

"What was that?" asked Kennedy abruptly.

Both men stiffened, both men pulled the pistols from their holsters. Something was coming towards them—something that was crawling noisily and clumsily through the long grass, something that made a spine-chilling whimpering sound as it crawled. The beams of two torches stabbed the darkness. They fell on a man—if George Tolliver could still be called a man. Something had mangled him dreadfully around the face and neck, so that it seemed a miracle that he was still living, still moving. He got somehow to his feet, glaring at Kennedy and Gladen with glazed eyes. He tottered.

It was Kennedy who conquered his revulsion, who made a step forward to catch him before he fell. Tolliver snarled, and leapt to meet him. It seemed that the long, yellow teeth were the only recognisable features in that ruined face.

It was Gladen who fired—who, standing a little to one side, poured a stream of the explosive slivers into the body of the madman. Tolliver was knocked backwards, away from Kennedy. He fell on his back. He twitched twice, then did not move again.

"Who . . . What did it?" stammered Kennedy. "It must have been some wild beast. But why should he turn on us?"

There was a scream from the lifeboat.

They ran across the rough ground, panting, stumbling. The airlock doors of the boat were open, a light was showing inside. Kennedy was first up the ladder, first to see the struggle that raged in the living compartment. Mrs. Tolliver was huge, and she was muscled like a man, like a strong man—but Susan Weldon, for all her apparent fragility, was no weakling. She was fighting for her life, fighting to keep the other woman's blood-smeared mouth from her throat. She could not spare the breath for any further outcry.

Kennedy did not hesitate. He knew, now, who it was that had almost killed George Tolliver, that had left him for dead. Moving fast, yet with a certain deliberation, he slid down the sloping deck, decreasing the range so that there would be no possible chance of his missing. He opened fire.

Then he was pulling the huge, heavy body of Mrs. Tolliver off Susan. Then the girl was in his arms, and he was kissing her desperately. He forgot Gladen. He forgot all those who had already died. All that was worth remembering, all that was worth knowing was in his arms.

It was Gladen who, at last, interrupted them, saying, "Get out of here, you two. I'll get the mess cleared up."

He had been in love before, and so had she. He had been in love before—but never before had he felt this aching intensity of desire. At times he almost wondered if it were entirely natural, but he did not let it worry him. Neither did it worry him that Gladen was doing all the work around the camp—tending the solar-power screen and the batteries, sending out the distress call at the scheduled times, even writing up the Log. At times he heard the rattle of the older man's typewriter, assumed that he was working off his frustrations by literary productivity.

Then came the morning when Kennedy and Susan, still in bed, heard the unmistakable crack of a Minetti automatic. Kennedy climbed into his shorts, picked up his own pistol and ran from the tent. Susan, throwing a light robe around herself, followed him. Everything was silent outside. Kennedy felt a chilly foreboding, walked slowly to the tent that had once been occupied by the Grants, that now housed Gladen.

Gladen was dead.

There was no doubt as to the cause of death—even just a single shot from a Minetti can lay bare the entire chest cavity, can expose the exploded heart among the wreckage of splintered ribs. The sight was not a pretty one.

"I'll handle this," said Kennedy shakily. "Get back to the tent, darling. I'll look after everything."

"But why?" she asked. "Why did he do it?"

"I can guess," replied Kennedy. "Perhaps, in his shoes, I'd have done the same."

"Need we have been so . . . selfish?" she said softly. "He must have been lonely."

She left him then, and he went

into the tent to do what had to be done.

Gladen's typewriter stood on a folding table. Beside it was a little pile of manuscript. A suicide note? wondered Kennedy. He walked to the table, picked up the top sheet. It was addressed to him with the words: RALPH, THIS IS FOR YOUR EYES ONLY. READ IT, THEN ACT AS YOU SEE FIT.

Kennedy picked up the second sheet.

"I'm a coward," he read, "to tell you what I have to tell you in this manner. But, perhaps, you would have paid no heed to me had I told you in any other way. It is certain that I'd never have been able to distract your attention from Susan had I not resorted to this somewhat drastic method. And it's *essential* that you know what all this is about. You're a responsible sort of bloke, and I can rely upon you to take action.

"I'll come to the point right away. *You're not immune.* Neither of you is immune. Nor am—was?—I. I thought that I was at first, that the three of us were,—but latterly my natural feelings of sexual jealousy have been augmented in a most frightening manner and I've been feeling a lust towards Susan that is quite foreign to my nature. My attitude towards sex has always been that I can take it or leave it; I've never cared much either way. Now I feel that I must have it—or else. *This* 'else', this way out that I am taking, is better than murder and rape.

"And still I haven't come to the point. I'd better waste no more time. The . . . The *thing* has reached the stage when it has to be passed on somehow, to somebody. The fact that the only available hosts are already fully occupied, are already busy infecting and re-infecting each other, doesn't matter. (Perhaps a certain mixing of the strains is part of the process.) Anyhow, I can recognize the symptoms in myself. I tried to drink a glass of water just now. (Remember poor Fuller and his tea?) There's the excessive salivation. (Remember that little bear-thing that we thought that Grant had killed?) There's the foreboding of impending dissolution. (That's not surprising—but I'm going to go out *my* way.)

"I did a lot of research for my last novel. It was historical—late Nineteenth Century. I wanted one of my characters to die rather messily, and in a way typical of the times, so I browsed through medical text books of the period and found all sorts of really fancy diseases that haven't been known for generations. The one that most appealed to me was rabies. It could almost have been made to measure for one of the malignant, intelligent viruses that the science fiction boys are always playing around with. The fascinating thing about it was the way in which it was passed on.

"Look at it this way. Consider malaria. It was a fever, and it was often fatal. It was carried from human host to human host by a little blood-sucking insect called the mosquito—which was a host itself. The mosquito, when feeding, pierced the victim's skin with its proboscis and, first of all, injected saliva into the tiny wound to dilute the blood. But this is the point. The micro-organism responsible for malaria was transmitted from one host to the next quite by chance and entirely by the normal gratification of the mosquito's normal appetite. The same could be said about typhus, transmitted from rat to man by another parasitical arthropod called the flea.

"Then there was syphilis, one of the so-called venereal diseases. It was transmitted from man to woman, and from woman to man, during coitus. Once again, only normal appetites were involved.

"With rabies, however, a strong element of the abnormal was involved. The disease affected the brain of the host—dogs were the most common carriers, although bats and other mammals were known to spread the infection—inducing a murderous frenzy. The afflicted animal would attack anything, everything and everybody in its path and the virus of the disease would be implanted into the wounds made by the animal's teeth, carried there by the abundant saliva. It was all very complicated. It was all far more complicated than the usual story of virus and vector, inasmuch as the vector was driven into utterly abnormal behaviour so that it could act as such.

"This local virus works on the same lines—or more so.

"The bear-thing bit Mrs. Grant. Mrs. Grant behaved in an utterly abnormal manner—yes, I'm sure that it was abnormal—with Fuller. She must have infected him, as well as her husband. (I don't think that with this virus the bite, the actual breaking of skin, is necessary; intimate contact is enough.) Then Fuller, when he attacked Tolliver, infected him. He, Tolliver, infected his wife. She, that night when she tried to seduce (or rape) me, infected me. Later she infected Susan, and she . . .

"But there's no need to write about it, Kennedy, and I'd sooner not.

"I'm almost finished now. I'll say what I have to say and then make my exit. Think about what I've said, Kennedy. Face facts. It looks as though you and Susan *will* be the Adams and Eve of a new race on this planet—and by all indications it will be a race of rapists and murderers. I may be wrong. It could be that some sort of symbiosis will work itself out over the generations, or some sort of immunty or near-immunity. Unluckily I'm no biologist, and neither are you.

"All I can say—selfishly—is that I'm glad that the responsibility is yours and not mine. I'm rather sorry that I shan't be around to see how you handle it."

"You bastard!" said Kennedy bitterly. Then—"I'm sorry, Gladen. You did right to tell me what you knew, what you guessed. You didn't tell me what to do—but that's not your job."

Moving mechanically he found a shovel, dug a grave just outside the tent. He pulled the shattered body out to the hole, rolled it in. He filled in the grave, stamped the loose earth down tight. He walked slowly to the river to wash.

I can feel the beginnings of it, he thought. The fear of water. How much is real, how much imagination after reading Gladen's testament? How long will Susan and I be able to carry on the way we are doing? Is our love—or lust—permanent, or will it give way to the other sort of lust? Shall I wake up one morning to find her teeth in my throat, or mine in hers?

The girl was waiting for him in the tent. He looked at her with coldly objective eyes. She was obviously pregnant. Would the child, he wondered, be born with the virus already in its blood or would the poison come from its mother's milk, its mother's kisses?

"Have you . . . ?" she asked.

"Yes," he said. "I've buried him."

"Poor Stephen," she said softly. "He must have been so very lonely. Did he leave any message?"

"No," said Kennedy.

"You're lying," she said.

He felt dislike—or was it more than dislike?—flare within his mind. She has the child, he thought. I've fulfilled my biological function. Will this cause her to hate me, to want to kill me, rather than to love me?

"What did he say?" she asked coldly.

"He left no message," repeated Kennedy.

What long teeth she has, thought Kennedy. And sharp . . .

"Why are you baring your teeth like that?" she asked.

"I can smile, can't I?" he snarled.

"What is there to smile about?" she demanded.

What, indeed? he thought. Do I kill the two of us—the three of us, rather—or do I kill just myself? Do I give her and the child a chance to live, incestuously to breed a race of monsters? Will they be monsters? Will the child be a boy? What chance is there that she and the child will survive when I am gone?

"Why is your face working so?" she asked. "Are you mad?"

"Yes. I am. And so are you."

"What do you mean?"

"How long is it since you had a bath? How much are you drinking these days?"

"What are you getting at?"

"Will you answer my questions?"

"Will you answer mine?"

She started to say something, but he never heard what it was. Everything was blotted out by a red haze of hate—hate such as he had never known could exist. There was a low growling sound in his ears; with faint surprise he realized that he was making it. He knew dimly that he was advancing on her with hands outstretched to clutch and rend, with bared teeth. Somebody screamed. He never knew if it was her, or himself.

Somehow she managed to evade his hands, pushed past him, ran clumsily out of the tent. Turning to follow, he tripped and fell. When he recovered his feet she was half way to the forest.

He ran in pursuit. It was like the dreams that he had sometimes about flying, it seemed that he was skimming over the grass with effortless ease. He was gaining, but not gaining fast enough. When he reached the trees he had lost sight of her.

"I must find her," he was muttering. "I must find her."

He ran on blindly, staggered back from a blow that felt as though it had pushed in his face. Raging, he attacked the tree against which he had blundered, then, with a return to something approaching sanity, fell back from the unyielding, insensate trunk and stood there, looking around him.

Something white caught his eye—it was a shred of material from her robe snagged on a thorn. A little further on there was another one. He growled again, with satisfaction. Again he started to run, but more cautiously, alert for further signs of her passage. The blood from his nose ran into his open, gasping mouth, mingled with the saliva running down his chin.

Something roared, but he paid it no heed. There were so many noises in his ears that one more meant nothing. He ran on, and on, ignoring the deep scratches scored into his unprotected skin by the thorny bushes, the occasional heavy blows that he sustained as he blundered into trees. Once or twice he lost the trail and cast around in circles, whining like a dog. He must find her. That was all he knew. He must find her.

He was out of the forest, under the open sky. The small part of his mind that retained some vestige of sanity told him that she must have circled, that she was making her way back to the camp. He saw her then, a white figure half way to the gleaming hemispheres of the tents.

She is going to escape in the boat, he thought. She mustn't. I must catch her and kill her before she reaches the boat.

She tripped and fell. She regained her feet, but he was on her. He caught her shoulders, pulled her round so that she was facing him. He ignored the clawed fingers that reached for his face, brought his mouth, his teeth down to the white neck in which a vein pulsed.

The noises in his ears were loud, but over them he heard her screaming. She struggled viciously. When, suddenly, she went limp he was taken unawares and almost dropped her.

A second later, just before he was able to sink his teeth in her neck, he did drop her, overwhelmed by a choking dizziness charged with rage and frustration, and fell beside her. He realized dimly, before he lost consciousness, that she had regained her knees, and now was bending over him.

"We thought we'd lost you," said the doctor. "The girl did a wizard job of nursing you, but you were still delirious when we landed—you were violent when we tried to get you aboard ship. We were all relieved when we were able to put you in the deep freeze."

Kennedy looked around the plainly furnished little cabin. He listened to the faint sounds—the whine and throb of machinery, the sound of feet on metal decks—that told of a ship in deep space. He looked at the elderly, uniformed man who was sitting by his bunk.

"I still can't believe it," he said. "Put me in the picture again, will you?"

The doctor smiled.

"We picked up your signals. Our navigator worked out where they were coming from. We proceeded straight to the planetary system indictated, threw ourselves into an orbit around the world on which you had landed, succeeded, with the aid of our detectors, in locating your boat. Nobody answered our signals, so our Captain decided that there must be something wrong and gave orders that our landing party carry arms—including, as you know, anesthetic gas grenades. Our boat landed by your camp, which appeared to be deserted. Then we saw you burst out of your tent, running like a mad thing, with Miss Weldon after you. We thought at first that you had seen or heard us landing and were hurrying to greet us. When you attacked us we were astounded. Then we managed to make sense of what Miss Weldon was shouting, and our third pilot, who was in charge of the boat, had the presence of mind to use the grenade thrower. You were lucky, too, that we had such a thing with us—if the Old Man hadn't had one broken out of the consignment of military equipment, and if we'd had only the usual lifeboat firearms, we'd have shot to kill. We could see even then that you had the human disease."

"The *what?*"

"Let me take it in order," the doctor said. "That manuscript we found in Gladen's tent gave us all the other clues we needed. You and the girl were rushed back to the ship—you partially recovered consciousness en route and gave us a lot of trouble, so we stashed you in my deep freeze. The Old Man gave me time to organize a hunting party. We caught six of those little bears,. two of which carried the virus. With the local fauna, by the way, it seems to work in cycles—love during the breeding season, hate at other times. But I had already deduced that, as soon as I'd run a complement-fixation test. It always works like that when there *is* a breeding season, but of course in man there isn't—or else the breeding season is year-round, take your pick of definitions."

"But it's fatal," Kennedy said.

"Not at all. It's quite self-limiting; the fatalities are inflicted by the victims on each other. And the severity of the disease depends on how it's transmitted. Miss Weldon got it purely through the mucous membranes—but you got it through a break in the skin. The latter is much the more virulent form; that's why she was able to recover faster than you did, and nurse you for a week before we landed. Mr. Gladen was wrong about that, and it's a doubly sad affair that he thought he had to kill himself. He probably never had the disease at all—after all, he was raised on Earth, and very probably was hyper-immune. His imagination betrayed him."

"Now that's enough hints," Kennedy said. "The human disease—Gladen raised on Earth—what are you driving at?"

"This *is* the human disease, Mr. Kennedy," the doctor said regretfully. "It is common to all Earth-like planets. Early man had a good immunity to it—it seldom made him overtly mad: he simply had these emotional seizures in the same way he had periodic colds. But most of humanity had been a long time off Earth, and the inherited immunity seldom lasts beyond the first six weeks of life. Six of you were push-overs for the virus; Mr. Gladen, very probably, was not.

"As for you, luck was with you. I had no anti-serum for the disease aboard, but I was able to prepare some from the two infected bears that we caught. As you see, it works." He chuckled. "You were like a patient out of time, Mr. Kennedy—a man suffering under a curse."

"What is the name of this disease?" Kennedy said in a smothered voice.

"The official name would mean nothing to you. The two syndromes it produces have the oldest names in the universe. Love and hate."

The cabin door opened.

"I heard that, doctor," said Susan. "But you produced only half a cure."

"I didn't use all the anti-serum," said the doctor, but neither Kennedy nor the girl heard him. He shrugged his shoulders and left the cabin.

Alyn knew that what she saw was an illusion. But who was to decide what was real—the natives, or the Earthmen?

WHEN THE SHOE FITS

by

James E. Gunn

ALYN WAS A XENOLOGIST. She was also a woman. The xenologist was worried. The woman was scared. The natives were throwing a ball, and she had a horrid suspicion that her teammates would insist she go.

She slipped through the market place, unnoticed in the blaze of noon, and damned private enterprise. . . .

Private enterprise made ET exploration possible. Government could do it, but Government wouldn't. That had been proved. Space was fantastically big, and ET exploration was fantastically expensive. ET exploration was also vital: humanity needed a frontier for the good of its soul; for the good of its body it needed that frontier as far as possible from Earth.

Laws were drafted to make exploration profitable, and humanity was unleashed upon the galaxy. *Jonathan Craddock, Exploiters and Importers,* was born—along with one hundred competitors, more or less.

The Bureau of Extraterrestrial Affairs was born at the same time to enforce the laws and regulate the profit.

If an exploration team located an uninhabited world or a Level 6 culture—stringently defined by BETA regulations as one ready for terrestrial contact—the company received an exclusive franchise to exploit that world. In actual practice only the Level 6 discovery was worthwhile. Exploitation of an uninhabited world was theoretically possible, but at this stage of Earth's technological development, the capital outlay was prohibitive. A company could wait five years for a profit; it couldn't wait a hundred.

On the other hand, one Level 6 discovery recouped a thousand failures. Virgin trade territory was fabulously profitable.

Exploration teams had two assets: the Fairfax field, that subtle electronic gadget which persuades those creatures within its range that they see what they are expecting to see; and the quality of their members, who were motivated by that most reliable of incentives—greed. Their rewards were graduated sharply according to achievements up to a Level 6 plateau which made each team member independently wealthy for life.

Labor unions objected to the incentive system; idealists objected to the motives. Both worked. The persons who signed company contracts sought not security but adventure, not ends but means. They were neither morally better nor worse than the ordinary run of humanity, but they were more determined, more persistent, more ingenious, and more trustworthy.

The teams had an equal number of debits: since the companies could not wait centuries, the teams had to move fast; and speed means mistakes through lack of understanding. Like idioms. The Translators were good, but only experience can translate idioms....

That thought bothered Alyn most as she threaded her way through the crowded street back toward the ship. A native turned sharply and looked at her with surprised violet eyes. Then she drew closer, and his eyes went blank. Alyn shivered, although Meissner's Star was hot, and drew her cloak closer around her.

"When there's dirty work to be done," she thought rebelliously, "I'm the one who has to do it."

Her lips moved silently, she damned them: Davis, Pip, and the Skipper—her teammates, her men, her children, her lovers....Long ago Earth's voyagers had found the ideal spaceship complement: three men and a woman. Carefully selected, a woman could easily be all things to three men, and three men, if they tried hard, could be all things to a woman.

But they imposed on her, as men do upon a woman who loves them. They expected her to slave for them all night and all day, too, while they lolled at home....

She focused her desires on reaching the spaceship that towered tall and iridescent in the distance. Home. They would be waiting for her. Her face softened, grew feminine and lovely. Quiet, loyal Davis—the methodical scientist, at home with things, asea in human rela-

---

JAMES E. GUNN first appeared in science-fiction in 1949 under a pseudonym, but in recent years the pen-name seems to have gone into semi-retirement. A prolific writer of short stories, Gunn is also the author of a novel, "This Fortress World" (Gnome Press).

tions, never expecting anything, always grateful for whatever he received. Little, effervescent Pip—the sure-fingered technician, shrewd, impertinent, and easily hurt. The Skipper—big, blond, self-sufficient, monosyllabic, avuncular. . . .

He was older than the others, Alyn thought, but not that old. She would have to be particularly attractive to him—

A native jostled her back to awareness. She almost screamed. Panicky, she clutched the cloak, hugged it tight. The Fairfax Field was a wonderful thing—it made xenological field work possible—but it was less deceptive in daylight. At the periphery, the natives were catching glimpses of her as she really was. Soon they would start putting the extraordinary together, and they would get "alien."

Then, at best, the Team would be out—with the Company on its back and the Bureau on its neck.

While she was about it, she damned the Company, too. It cut a corner, saved a penny, and lost a world. These Field generators were obsolescent, and she was getting a bounce effect that made her observations virtually worthless. It was all very well for the natives to see her as a native and the Ship as a native dwelling, but when she saw their world as vaguely Earth-like, the whole enterprise became pointless. It was impossible to tell what was real and what was Fairfax. . . .

The town was an 18th century English village trembling perilously on the brink of the Industrial Revolution . . . but not quite.

The picture was just a little askew, as if the signboard of the village inn illustrated a beheading with half a dozen natives lying, mouths open, to catch the blood as it fell.

As a matter of fact, that *was* the signboard of the village inn. It was, apparently, an idiom—or, at least, the way in which Alyn's mind, reinforced by the bounce effect of the Fairfax Field, interpreted the native idiom. Probably it was not that at all.

So it went. The houses were not quite the proper shape. They were built solidly enough of bricks or stone, but they were painted with intricate, painstaking, many-colored designs.

She came out of the market place into the green common. She threaded her way between grazing ruminants that were not quite cows and restrained an impulse to run. She walked down a street that was not quite cobblestone among creatures that were not quite human.

They were man-shaped, but their torsos were too long and oddly distorted, pigeon-breasted, as if there were too many bones inside. Their arms were short, and their hands had only four fingers, like cartoon characters. Their heads were small and their faces malformed, with pushed-in noses, large, bulging violet eyes, wide mouths and pointed teeth, and prognathous jaws.

They looked like hairless Pekingese dogs, a caricature of humanity that made Alyn want to scream.

Their name for themselves translated as "the People." The Team called them "Pekes," against all rules—BETA, Company, and scientific. By extension, Meissner's Star (2) became "Peking."

The Pekes made Alyn nervous. She didn't mind creatures that scampered or writhed or swam or oozed, but she couldn't stand creatures who walked on two legs and looked her in the eye. If they weren't human, they gave her the willies.

They were humanoid—the Fairfax Field couldn't falsify that. And that was just what made any conclusions dangerous.

Alyn scrambled up the ladder. The spaceship door swung open. She walked through the air lock, went through the inner door, and climbed the stairway to the living deck.

Davis turned from his workbench, a test tube forgotten in his fingers. Pip looked up from the delicately carved lapis lazuli he was examining through a loupe. The Skipper swung down from the bridge. They looked at her expectantly, a little greedily.

Alyn said, "They're going to have a ball."

She let the cloak and hood slip down. It crumpled on the floor. Underneath it she was wearing a halter and shorts. She had a good figure—slim and youthful, but womanly.

She had the type of face that is best described as fascinating. Partly it was her red hair, but it was more the face: forehead too high, cheekbones too prominent, lips too firm, chin too stubborn, eyes too intelligent. They made a combination men found irresistible, but she was too sane to make it her fortune.

Perhaps that was why she had joined *Jonathan Craddock*. Or maybe it was the money. Nowhere else could a woman retire at thirty, unencumbered, with enough money to let her do what she wished for the rest of her life—if her team were lucky enough to hit upon that one-in-a-hundred Level 6 culture.

Or maybe it was because only with *Jonathan Craddock*—or a competitor—could she practice legalized polyandry. Had she, as woman always had, followed the interesting men, the voyagers, the risk-takers? It was a question she had been unable to answer for herself. She knew only that the ones left at home were culls.

"Careful with that cloak," Davis said absently. "There's ten thousand bucks worth of Fairfax Field wired into that rag."

Alyn scowled at him. "And it doesn't work. I'm getting too much bounce effect." She shrugged and turned away. "No matter, anyhow. No more daylight work for me. It's too hot in that cloak, and too dangerous."

Pip chuckled. "Trust the incredulity factor, Alyn."

"Don't blabber."

But Pip was probably right. That was how the Field worked. Or how it was thought to work; there was a lot of disagreement. Fairfax himself had always insisted that it did no more than satisfy the brain's visual scanning mechanism, the alpha rhythm; it stopped—or interfered with—the scanning sweep, giving the watcher the sense of seeing something without specifying what that something was. From there on, the incredulity factor took over—that habit of the mind which directs it to seek always the simpler explanation. That there are aliens among us is a wild fantasy; it is simpler to assume that what one sees is something ordinary, seen badly.

But not every mind has an alpha rhythm to interrupt—for instance, M-types. Some epistomologists doubted that the Field affected the mind at all, and photographs supported them: an object inside a Fairfax Field *was* optically blurred, even to the mindless eye of a camera. But if that were all there was to it, why the bounce effect—and the critical tuning that made it possible to get rid of it?

"I don't think it's just the incredulity factor," Alyn said slowly. "The Pekes are just humanoid enough to make us forget that they're aliens. But *we're* the aliens; *we* don't expect to see something ordinary here, unless the Field is leaking. And I think it is. It rattles me, Pip."

"The ball," the Skipper prompted.

Alyn started. "That's what the Translator called it. A dance with music. If they dance and if they have music. Maybe it's a party where they play footsie and later pay the piper. Who can be sure with an idiom?"

"Who's throwing it?" Davis asked.

"The king, chief, elder, headman —whatever you want to call him. If he's any of those. We can't overestimate our inability to translate accurately."

"Understood," the Skipper said impatiently.

"Well," Alyn continued reluctantly, "he lives in that big pile of masonry on the hill above town. He's got a male offspring—or maybe it's an heir designate from the village—anyway, he's come of age, and the king has invited all the nubile maidens in the kingdom to a ball at which the prince will take his pick. For what purpose I can only guess. It isn't even safe to guess...." She looked at the Skipper and read something in his eyes which made her look quickly at Pip and even quicker at Davis. "No," she said weakly, and then more defiantly, "No! NO! I won't do it. You can't make me do it!"

"Big chance," the Skipper pointed out. "Ceremony. Good evidence."

"You're the woman," Pip said, "and the xenologist."

"It's now or never," Davis added.

"Then it's never," Alyn said breathlessly. "Mixing with Pekes at an affair like that! Anything might happen. My cloak could be pulled away. . . ."

Pip reassured her. "I'll take care of that."

"Let's give up on Peking. We're wasting our time. It'll never pay out. The Pekes aren't Level 6 or even Level 5. Anyway, they've got nothing worth exporting."

"Maybe," the Skipper said, shrugging. "Still a chance."

"There's the jewels and the engravings," Davis said.

"Al's right," Pip said. "We can't collect enough secretly to make it worthwhile. Extra-T curios are scarcely worth hold space, anyhow. But Level 6! You never can tell about the Bureau. Tell the truth, Al. Why don't you want to go to the ball?"

She burst into tears of weariness and frustration. "Because I've got nothing to wear, stupid!"

"Is that all?" Pip said slyly.

"Last chance," the Skipper said bluntly.

Alyn snapped, "Well, why don't one of you go?"

"Oho!" Pip chortled. "The Field is good, but not good enough to turn us into nubile maidens. It will have to work hard enough on you."

"You're hateful!" Alyn snapped, stamping her foot. "When we get back, one of us can just find another group, that's all!"

"She'll go," said the Skipper.

Alyn came out of her cabin with a swish and a swirl of musical white crinoline that made three masculine jaws drop in admiration. She was a creature of elegance and radiant beauty, from her transparent shoes to her living crown of coiled hair sparkling with tiny stars. She was every man's desire. . . .

Pip recovered first. "You've got the Field turned on!"

"Say, now," Davis protested. "We've got to live with you, you know. That's not fair."

"Right," the Skipper said.

Alyn pivoted on her right heel and faded. Not much. Just enough to appear only humanly desirable. "Serves you right. You're mean, sadistic beasts, all of you, and I don't know why I ever signed on." She looked down at her dress, spun slowly around, and couldn't sustain a frown. She sighed. "It's beautiful."

For once all of them were silent. Finally Davis said, "We wanted to give you a present."

Pip added softly, "We saved it for a moment when you needed it most."

"Surprise," said the Skipper.

Alyn's frown returned. "And you gave it to me now so that I'd do your dirty work for you. Men!" She turned sharply on Pip. "The reason I turned on the Field—I had to try it out. And I got a frightful bounce effect."

Pip grinned. "We looked good to you, too, huh? Well, it figures. A small unit like that one in the heel of your right shoe can't carry much shielding. It's not centrally located either. A marvelous piece of micro-machining, though. Worth its weight in tickets home. One thing—the battery is good for only four hours. Be back before then."

"It's battery operated?" Alyn exclaimed.

"Just the receiver. The Field itself is picked up from the ship. Don't worry—as long as you get back within four hours."

"Fine, wonderful," Alyn muttered. "Eight-nine-ten-eleven-twelve. Pip isn't this a little thick? Who do you think you're fooling with this fairy tale?"

Pip looked sheepish. "It's a gamble."

"You lost. I won't go."

Davis protested, "But there's no time to change our plans."

"Right," said the Skipper. "Pip's sorry. No difference. Must go."

"Fairy tale themes are endlessly repetitive," Pip said. "The good ones, anyway. That's why they persist. They express something fundamental about existence." After a moment he added: "We'll be there too, you know."

Alyn's face softened. "I might have known you wouldn't toss me out completely on my own. Who's going to carry the camera?"

"I—" Davis began, and stopped.

Alyn took a deep breath. "Okay. Don't drop it. I don't know where I'm going, but I'll want to know where I've been—and who I was at the time."

She made her way down the treads to the air lock and through it and down the ladder to the ground as carefully as a conductor threading his way through an orchestra-pit. The dress was an encumbrance, but it was also a necessity. She would have been better off in a cloak, but she would never have gone in a cloak.

Behind her came Davis and Pip. To her they looked like Davis and Pip in hood and cloak. To Pekes they would look like Pekes—perhaps. That was the beauty of the Fairfax Field: it reinforced the expected image.

Or did it? Suppose the Pekes were M types, *Minus* the alpha rhythm, wholly visual thinkers whose minds were so busy manipulating images that they had no scanning pattern to interrupt? Or suppose they were P-for-Persistent types, wholly abstract thinkers, whose alpha rhythm went on constantly without their feeling any need to satisfy it? Fairfax had been wrong, he had to be wrong. The field, had he been right, should work only for R-for-Responsive types, whose visual scanning stopped when they actually saw something, or their brains threw up a visual thought that substituted for an actual sighting. That would explain the disagreement on how it worked, for human beings were a mixed lot–mostly R.

If the Pekes were a mixed lot too, that left only the incredulity factor—quite unreinforced, except by the optical effect of the Field. It was not much to lean on.

She walked along the streets that were not quite cobblestone streets in her dancing slippers, one heel of which contained a Fairfax Field receiver and amplifier. The street was immaculate. That was one point for the Pekes—they were clean, unlike the pseudo-England she was seeing through the Field. . . . She stopped herself. Comparisons of that kind were the xenologist's pitfall; the use of the Field prohibited them. Too much bounce effect.

Just once she looked back at the ship. To her it looked like a ship—a wonderful shiny fortress of a ship, but still a ship. To the Pekes—perhaps—it looked like a native fortress that had been there ever since they could remember.

Providing the Pekes were all R's—*and* providing that the Field had anything at all to do with the alpha rhythm.

There was scarcely anyone on the street: a few late shoppers hurrying home, a policeman sauntering along, checking the stores. . . .

A policeman!

He saw Alyn and smiled. "Ah, there," he said in a rich Irish brogue, "anither maiden for the ball, is it? You'd better be hurrying, me dear, or the Prince will have made his pick and you not there."

Alyn shivered. She was getting a bounce effect to end all bounce effects. A policeman, indeed! She bent her head and moved rapidly toward the large building on the hill.

As she drew near, it looked more like a palace than the native structure she remembered. She climbed the gleaming marble stairs and passed between tall columns to the big, brass doors. They swung open. A uniformed majordomo bowed her into a long hallway carpeted in red velvet. Its walls were hung with tapestries. . . . Tapestries!

She turned to run away, panic fluttering like a bird in her throat. But she glimpsed Davis and Pip skulking behind. They wouldn't let her quit. What they had, the Team, was based on confidence. Once it was shattered, the Team was broken, no good, and what they had was no good either. . . .

She turned back to the hallway.

It led her into a magnificent ballroom, its dark, parquet floor glistening in the light of dozens of candelabra hanging from the vaulted ceiling. The floor was crowded with beautiful women and handsome men, all dressed to the teeth, bejeweled and bespangled. They danced to the music of an orchestra that played on a distant platform.

As she hesitated, the dancers stopped. The music died away. Everyone's eyes turned toward her. Panic surged into her throat again. She bit her lower lip to keep from screaming.

Out of the throng came a man moving slowly, his dark eyes fixed upon her face. He was a tall man, broad-shouldered and lean, his face ruggedly handsome, his mouth betraying an unsuspected sensitivity. He wore a Graustarkian uniform, sparkling with buttons, jingling with medals. . . .

He was—the dream prince, the fairy tale prince, the answer to every maiden's prayer. . . . And he was just as real.

Still, Alyn could not resist a shiver of anticipation as he approached her. His eyes searched her face until he was very close; her knees got a little weak. His hand reached out for hers. He bowed low over it. His lips kissed her palm. For a frantic moment she thought of the Pekes' needle-sharp teeth. . . .

Her last really sane thought was: *How does this look to Davis and Pip. . .? What is really happening?*

Then she surrendered herself to the illusions of the Fairfax Field and the arms of the Prince.

The ballroom floor was like an undersea fairyland of color and music through which she swam like an infinitely graceful angelfish around which the Prince pirouetted and returned in a hypnotic mating dance. Around her moved other dancers. Music played distantly, something familiar although she could not quite place it. But neither one made any real impression upon her.

She had no eyes for anyone but the Prince, no ears for anything but his whispers. What did he say? Nothing and everything—she could not remember, and yet it was what should have been said, what had to be said. . . . She knew that at the time. Nothing was done to break the spell—for it was a spell; she knew it, and she could not change it, and she would not have changed it if she could.

She was falling in love. She was falling in love with a Peke, with a creature impossibly alien. She knew it and it didn't matter.

This was not like the love she felt for Davis and Pip and the Skipper. That had been an emotion slow in developing, even slower in being recognized for what it was: an emotion compounded of the maternal, the protective, the tolerant, and the sexual.

This was a love of another color. This was romantic love, a scarlet thing. The Prince was perfection;

his touch made her faint. Life was bliss that would never end, a fire that raced through her veins, a tide that choked her throat, a delicious ache that turned her limbs languorous. . . .

She was in love with a dream, with a Field-induced delusion, but now it didn't matter. The emotion alone was enough.

Time passed like a blurred watercolor. She was delirious, feverish, enraptured, abandoned, reckless. . . . The Prince led her toward a small doorway, his hand holding hers, his eyes fixed upon her face. She followed dreamily. Wherever her Prince led, she would follow. His dear face preceded her, the cute, little upturned nose, the violet eyes, the wide, sensitive mouth. . . .

"Alyn!"

Someone was calling her. Who? No matter. Nothing mattered but the Prince.

"Alyn! Alyn! Alyn! Alyn! . . ." It went on like that, like the tolling of a bell. She couldn't ignore it; somehow she would have to silence it.

Her eyes cleared a little. Out of the surrounding blur came a face she knew. It was Pip's face. It was contorted, the mouth open, yelling at her. . . .

"Alyn! For crimeny's sake, the battery's failing. You're coming through. We've got to get out of here. What's the matter with you? Snap out of it! Alyn!"

The mists thinned. Her eyes swept the faces around her: Peke faces. Even the Prince's face was a Peke's face, beloved though it was. . . .

Sanity returned like a cold sea wave engulfing her. She would have to run. She turned wildly and fled through the hall. No longer was it a ballroom. It was a big, rough masonry meeting room filled with Pekes. The candelabra were open gas flames.

The Pekes gaped at her. They couldn't be seeing her clearly yet. But they could see that she was acting strangely. Soon they would try to stop her.

Behind her a Peke voice called out. The Prince. She knew it instinctively. Her heart turned over, but still she ran.

She reached the doorway. The tapestries were really the intricate Peke designs drawn upon the walls. The red velvet carpet was a rush mat. Her shoe caught in it. She almost fell, but her foot pulled free, and she ran on.

At the big front door the Peke guard looked at her with startled eyes, but he wasn't quick enough to catch her. She was through the rough, board doorway and into the pebbled street, racing through the night toward the ship. . . .

Halfway there Pip caught up. He threw his cloak around her, and they ran together, side by side.

"Pip!" she sobbed gratefully. "Oh, Pip! What happened, Pip?"

"That's what I was going to ask

you. That Peke waltzed up to you like you were his one true love, and you went into those damn' arms of his like you knew it. He started stamping around you, and you stood there, turning slowly to face him, smiling. . . . Gosh, we were scared!"

"Where's Davis?" Alyn said in sudden alarm.

"He wanted to film the Pekes' reaction to your flight," Pip said quickly.

"You mean," Alyn said, panting, "he was going to head them off if they got too close. You're wonderful, you and Davis. I couldn't have better teammates." *Teammates, team mates. . . . But what about her soul mate? What about the Prince?*

She hadn't answered Pip's questions, but then he hadn't asked any. Not directly. They were there, close to his lips, and she couldn't answer them. What she had been through was too real, too emotionally meaningful. She was still shaken.

Suddenly she said, "Pip! I lost my shoe!"

"Which shoe?"

"The right shoe. The one with the unit in it!"

Pip pulled them to a stop. "We've got to get it back!"

But the hill was black with Pekes swarming after them like bees out of a disturbed hive. Pip muttered, "Maybe Davis picked it up." And they ran again.

Eventually, long after Alyn had decided it would be easier to let the Pekes catch her than to draw another tortured breath, they reached the ship. They scrambled into it, and they waited.

For hours the Pekes milled through the streets, searching for the impossible creatures who had impossibly disappeared. After they gave up, Alyn, Pip, and the Skipper waited for Davis. And waited, not talking. And waited, afraid to hope.

Just before dawn, he walked in, unruffled. They met him at the air lock.

"Wow!" Davis said as he slipped out of his cloak and carefully hung it up. "They were ready to bite each other's heads off. Did, as a matter of fact. The Prince acted like someone had hit him in the head with an axe."

Alyn watched his face intently, her green eyes unreadable.

Impatiently, Pip said, "Did you get the shoe?"

"What shoe?" Davis asked blankly.

They sat around the living deck, three men and a woman, waiting for something to happen. Pip fiddled with a micro-mechanism, doing more damage than good. Davis pretended to be interested in some tests he was running on an ore sample, but his gaze kept drifting toward the window. The Skipper leaned back in his favorite chair, his hands thrust deep into his pockets, not talking at all. Alyn sat in the window seat, staring at the street below.

"What I can't understand," Davis said suddenly, not looking at Alyn, "is why she was going into that room with that Peke."

"That's why I was there," Alyn said absently; "to find out everything I could."

"We didn't really intend for that to cover the possibility of cross-breeding," Pip said slyly. "Logically, this should be reported to the Bureau of Extraterrestrial Affairs."

"Don't be ridiculous," Alyn said, but her heart wasn't in it.

"You knew, of course," Pip went on, his eyes studying Alyn intently, "that it was a symbolic marriage. After consummation, the bride is sacrified as the repository of the bridegroom's youthful sins. He heads into manhood with a clean slate."

"What I can't understand," Davis said plaintively, "is how you expected to get out of that room."

"Maybe she didn't want to get out," Pip said slowly. "And now the Prince is searching for her throughout the land."

Alyn turned sharply on Pip. "What's that?"

"He's got that shoe of yours. He's sent it around to all the workmen in the village to see if they made it." Pip got up and walked to the window. He stared out. "He's trying to find you, Al."

Alyn's green eyes searched Pip's face.

"Let's get out of here!" Davis exploded. "We've fouled this one up completely."

"No!" Alyn said.

"Why?" said the Skipper.

Alyn said flatly, "I changed my mind."

"Can't anyway," said the Skipper. "Bureau would quarantine Peking. Bar Company for good. Company'd fire us. No good. Two chances: Pekes Level 6 or get back shoe."

Pip said to Alyn, "Good thinking!"

"Shut up!" Alyn snapped.

"What's the matter with everybody?" Davis asked in bewilderment. "Nobody's been himself since the ball. Alyn" — he flushed — "hasn't been friendly. Pip has been picking on her. The Skipper hasn't said a word. What's the matter?"

Nobody answered him. Pip shrugged, stared out the window, and began whistling *After the Ball Is Over*.

"We're waiting for the end of the story," Alyn said.

"And here he comes now," Pip said.

"Where?" Alyn said harshly.

Pip pointed. "See where he comes with the shoe in his hand."

The Peke marched steadily, purposefully toward the ship.

"Get this on film!" the Skipper snapped.

Davis sprang to the control room ladder.

The Peke got closer, became foreshortened, and passed beneath the curve of the ship. They waited, breathless. Davis backed down the ladder. They whirled on him and then turned back to their vigil.

The slow rasp of wood against metal drifted up to them. The Peke was climbing the ladder. The ship vibrated. Something rapped against the air lock door.

"Well?" Pip said.

Impassively, the Skipper said, "Let it in."

A little, involuntary wail broke from Alyn's lips. "I can't." She turned blindly and ran to her room. "Pip," she called back over her shoulder, "lock the door on that side."

She slammed the door behind her, slid the bolt across, and waited, her hand on it, until she heard the bolt outside click shut. It echoed in the little room with a grim finality. She threw herself onto her bunk and bit the pillow to keep from screaming.

Distantly she heard the air lock opened below and then the slow clomp of feet on stair treads. Voices rumbled for a long time. Once she found herself at the door, her hand on the bolt, before she remembered that it was bolted on the other side, too.

She threw herself back onto the bunk.

Time dripped slowly in discreet seconds. Hours later the ship vibrated again. This time the feet were descending. The air lock opened and closed and feet went down the ladder outside. Someone pounded at the door.

"Alyn!" Davis shouted. "We've got it. The Skipper swears it will stand up in every court in the galaxy. It's Level 6."

Slowly, wearily, Alyn got up and went to the door. When she opened it, Davis was there, his face flushed and triumphant. He caught her around the waist, lifted her, swung her around, shouting, "Let's celebrate. We're rich, we're rich!"

Finally he lowered her to the floor. Alyn said, "What happened?"

Pip said, "He figured it out. The Prince. The reports came back to him: none of the village workmen had made that unit in the slipper. None of them had ever seen anything like it. They could duplicate it, but they couldn't have invented it. Q.E.D.—aliens.

"He had the whole village questioned, the results tabulated and compared, the discrepancies noted. Then he came here."

"Alone?" Alyn asked. "Unarmed?"

Davis said happily, "He wants more gadgets like that one. They do magic. He's ready to trade."

"What has he got to trade?" Alyn asked sharply.

Pip said, "Skill. Peking is a mine of micro-skills waiting to be refined. They've been developing them for centuries with that intricate design work. All the Pekes need is a few simple tools and they can duplicate any micro-mechanism. They're quick, smart, accurate. I told you that Fairfax Field micro-unit was worth its weight in tickets home – well, his workmen had made *ten* of them already."

"But the Pekes aren't Level 6," Alyn objected.

"If deducing our presence from the shoe and locating us through comparative interviews isn't Level 6," Davis said, "there isn't a CQ test worth the computer it's figured in."

The Skipper rumbled, "Proof, too. On film. Rich. All of us."

Alyn bit her full lower lip. "What—did he say—about me?"

Slowly, watching her face, Pip shook his head. "He didn't mention you. But he left this." He tossed Alyn the slipper.

She caught it without thinking and then turned it over slowly to look at it from all sides.

"The foot the shoe fitted," Pip said gently, "was his." Pip's eyes were unusually quiet and dark.

Alyn nodded gravely and turned slowly back toward her cabin.

Davis stopped smiling. "What's the matter with her?"

Pip shook his head impatiently.

"What I can't understand," Davis whispered, "is why she wanted her door locked from this side when the Peke was here."

Pip said softly, "She wasn't afraid the Peke was coming after her. She knew he was. She was afraid he would ask her to go with him, and she wouldn't be able to refuse."

"Go with a Peke!" Davis exclaimed.

"With a Prince," Pip said.

Alyn hesitated at the door. "Let's get out of here!" she said harshly. "We got what we came after. Let's get back to Earth."

Pip said, "And so they lived happily ever after."

Cinderella cried half the long way home.

ATQUE VALE

Henry Kuttner died at Santa Monica, Calif., of a heart attack, February 6, 1958. The loss of this witty, humane and dedicated writer will grieve everyone who knew him, whether in person, through the mails, or in print. At his death, (he was only 43) he left behind at least 200 stories and more than a score of novels, both under his own name and his huge roster of pen-names (including Lewis Padgett, Laurence O'Donnell and C. H. Liddell).

Our condolences to his wife, C. L. Moore, who merged her own great gifts with his to produce much of the major work of the Kuttners.—JB

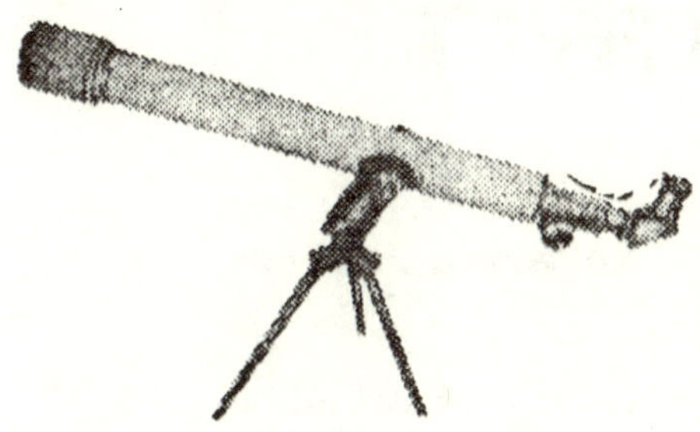

No dreamy, impractical artists are wanted in a steel mill. Not, that is, unless what you want is — SuperSteel.

THE STRAD EFFECT

by

Raymond F. Jones

HELL MUST EASILY BE as beautiful as Heaven, John Ward thought. At least, if a flowing stream of pure, molten steel is any symbol of Hell's hot fury.

He touched the crane controls with a gentle movement, upending a trifle more the massive ladle from which the white stream of steel emptied into the last of the moulds. It splashed over the edge as the mould filled to the top, and ran momentarily in a million points of fire on the pouring floor.

But the ladle was empty and this was the end of the shift. John Ward righted the ladle and swung it high, rolling the entire crane on its track to the end of the room. He turned off the power and tucked his glasses in his back pocket. He snapped his gloves together in his left hand, and filled out the day's log.

He glanced at the still-glowing moulds as he climbed down the ladder to the floor. This was going to be a good batch of steel, he thought. The best ever.

Intermountain Steel was a small outfit as steel companies go. But what it lacked in size it made up in vigor. It had an engineering department that believed steel was still as crude as clay, compared with what it ought to be in hardness and tensile strength. It had an advertising department that believed steel could be sold like cigarettes on TV, and it had a president, Jack Cochran, who believed in letting men do what they had enthusiasm for.

That's why Intermountain had a laboratory that would have done credit to a plant four times its size. Chief Test Engineer Mike Willard believed in production controls that had teeth.

When he went out for lunch he glanced through the glass panels of the lab where technician Wade Beck sat hunched on a high stool beside the giant hydraulic stress machine. Willard remembered that Beck had been sitting exactly that way at ten a.m.

When the Test Engineer came back from lunch the technician still had not moved. Willard entered the lab.

"You posing for a life study or something? You've been on that stool since ten o'clock this morning!"

Beck looked up, then slowly handed a clip board with a figure covered sheet to his Chief. "It's not easy for a man to admit he's slipping off his rocker."

Willard glanced at the figures. "There's something wrong with the machine."

Beck shook his head. "I've checked it over a dozen times. I've switched gauges until I've used every one in the place. They all check to the umpteenth place."

Willard clapped him on the shoulder. "Take off for lunch and come back this afternoon. You'll find the bug." He sighed thoughtfully. "This would be wonderful if it were true—a steel with a tensile strength eighty thousand pounds higher than the best we've ever turned out of this shop before."

"That gives me an idea!" Beck exclaimed. "I'm going to run some of our old stock, just to check on the machine. Maybe there is something new here!"

"Not that new. We'll have to send out for some gauges if you don't find the trouble soon. We want those tests by tomorrow forenoon. But go on out for lunch now, and clear the cranium."

Beck ignored the advice. He went to the stock room and got some samples of cold rolled rod from the batch he had tested two days before. He inserted the sample in the stress machine and stepped behind the shield to turn the power on.

Slowly, the needles of the gauges advanced as the stress increased. Beck watched it edge toward the normal reading for that type of metal. He glanced up once at the bar that was gradually thinning under the tremendous tension drawing it apart.

And then it snapped with a singing whine. Beck glanced at the graph that plotted the peak stress. It stood exactly at the point recorded for the batch two days ago.

He paused, his breath coming more heavily now. There was nothing wrong with the gauges. He was sure of that.

Swiftly, he replaced the sample with another specimen from the batch he'd been testing all morning. Behind the shield once again, he watched the tension mount. It crawled to the level at which the previous rod had broken—and was still going.

He watched it climb. Ten thousand pounds higher. Twenty. He peered out at the rod, which had thinned a little, but showed no signs of breaking yet. He leaned back, refusing to participate in the test with his personal reflexes any longer. He moved only once to reset the pen of the recorder as it moved off scale, as it had been doing all morning.

Then, at an incredible eighty-two thousand pounds above the previous reading, he heard the thin, screaming note of the parting steel.

There was nothing wrong with the machine or the gauges. They had a steel like no steel that had ever been seen before.

Jack Cochran was there, and Mike Willard. Thompson, and Manning, two of the floor foremen stood in the background. Pete Roberts, head of Sales, was moving around the desk, feeling one sample after another, as if some kind of magic would rub off on his own hands from the precious stuff. His eyes were glowing.

Wade Beck was describing for the twentieth time the sequence of tests and their results. This was a matter of form; all the others had witnessed some tests.

"When we announce this in the trade," Pete Roberts said excitedly as Beck finished, "there's going to be some reshuffling at the top of the pile. Little old Intermountain is going to tell U.S. Steel and some of the other boys to move over. We can charge our own price for this, and customers will be standing in line. A decrease in tonnage will make it compare in total cost with what they've already been using, but they'll be coming to Intermountain for a better product!"

"The patent department will have to consider this, first," said Cochran mildly.

"Look," Willard exclaimed in weariness. "Can't you get it through your heads that we have nothing to patent? We have nothing to sell! This thing is a freak. We don't know how this steel was made. We don't know if we can ever make another batch like it."

"Let me look at those logs again," Cochran asked Thompson.

The foreman passed them over and Cochran turned the pages slowly for the dozenth time. He shook his head. "There seems to be absolutely no variation in the charge that went into the furnace

---

RAYMOND F. JONES has been turning out speculative fiction since 1941. A former radio engineer and present government meteorologist, he specializes in "pure" s-f, in which all the facts are straight and the central dramatic actor is the idea. He is the author of two adult novels, "Renaissance" and "This Island Earth"; the latter was made into a movie. He has also written a teen-age novel, "The Secret People" (Avalon Books).

on those shifts. Are you sure you personally watched these charges and they looked normal to you?"

Thompson nodded. "Not a cinder went into that furnace that wasn't strictly according to Hoyle. It was charged just like I've been charging furnaces for twenty years. You can't blame me."

"We're not blaming you," Cochran said with a wry smile. "We'd like to credit you with discovering something no steelman has ever seen before. But we seem to have a complete mystery on our hands. A new steel, stronger than anything of its kind in history. And nobody knows how it was made!"

"What does that matter?" Pete Roberts said. "As long as we've got it we can sell it!"

"How do you know you'll ever get another batch like this?" Willard demanded angrily.

"Why shouldn't we?" Roberts' eyes were wide and innocent. He left production problems to those who understood them. "Nobody knows what keeps his own heart ticking—but he keeps on using it as long as he can and doesn't worry because he knows it's going to stop. I say let's sell this stuff while it's coming out."

"We've certainly got something here that we could market," Cochran said soberly, "if we knew we had a constant supply. But I'm inclined to agree with Willard. We ought to know more about what made this batch different, before we make any announcement, even to our own Directors. Continue the production tests," he said to Willard, "and stockpile any more that comes out like this. After a week or so we'll see what it looks like and go from there. Be sure you get a double check on every charge that goes in. We want to know exactly what this stuff is made of even if we don't know how."

It gave Willard a kind of perverse satisfaction that the next batch tested was entirely normal. By some incredible fluke, he thought, they had been given a glimpse into a kind of metallurgical heaven. But now the heavens were closed and they could expect no more visions like this.

The batch after that tested ninety-one thousand pounds per square inch above normal.

They instituted a weighing and watching procedure that measured the charges going into the furnaces down to the last gram. They had all logs triple checked and signed. No one's observations were to be trusted without verification.

It seemed to make no difference which of the four furnaces was involved. During the next two weeks there were batches that tested high in tensile strength, and there were batches that tested normal. And both kinds came from all the furnaces.

At the end of the second week,

Cochran reviewed the reports as a second conference was called. "It's baffling," he said, "but it looks as if we've got something we can count on. About one third of our production of steel is high tensile strength. The production curve seems to be regular—in its own spotty way."

"Then we can start a sales campaign right away?" Roberts asked.

"I'm inclined to favor it, on the basis that we are offering the results of new and limited production methods. Don't try to build it too big to start with. It's a risky thing to be doing, without any more knowledge than we've got. But on the other hand, it would be senseless not to sell what we've got for what it is."

"I'm against it," Willard said. "It's completely crazy. We can't go to steel users and tell them we've got something to sell that may be cut off any minute."

"We can't go on stockpiling this much of our production indefinitely," said Cochran. "It's either sell it for what it is, or push it out with the rest of our production without saying anything about it. That doesn't make very good sense either, does it?"

Willard shook his head. "I don't know the answer. I only know we're caught no matter which way we move."

He had to admit that Roberts' production was a masterpiece of the advertiser's misguided art. "Out of the Crucible of Superior Scientific Effort Comes the Miracle of a Metallurgical Milestone!"

His ads went on with quite a description of the sweat and blood of Intermountain Steel's scientific staff which had gone into the making of SuperSteel, his name for their unexpected miracle. He backed it up with charts and tables of the tests they had run.

The result was literally instantaneous. The office was swamped with orders for the new steel, and the laboratories were swamped with scientific inquiries concerning their methods of production.

The patent department was no happier about the situation than Willard was, but they had to admit you couldn't patent something you didn't know how you made. Everybody kept quiet on the subject. The scientists were put off with the story that the production methods were not ready to be revealed for legal reasons.

At the end of three days the stockpile of SuperSteel was depleted, and orders were being taken on a rationing basis for future production.

Willard knew they were sitting on a pile of dynamite. And the same day they shipped the last ton of SuperSteel from the yard his worst fears came true.

Out of a full twenty-four hours' production there was not an ounce of SuperSteel.

They stayed up all night watching the next runs. Nothing had changed in the routine. Nobody said anything to anybody. They just watched.

When batches were finally prepared for testing, out of those runs, they were all present once more. There was still little conversation except about the weather and the Yanks' batting. In silence they watched the needles and the graphs as Beck and Willard put in the samples and applied the stress. Every one snapped at normal limits.

"It looks like we've had it," Willard said. "It was a good thing while it lasted. Now all we need is a digestive system that can handle crow for a good, long time."

"Nuts!" Roberts snapped. "You guys are engineers. You're supposed to know how steel is made. You made SuperSteel once. You can do it again. Where's the guts of this outfit?"

Cochran smiled tolerantly. "I'm afraid this is one case where the pep talk and the old college try won't do, Pete. We know everything that went into SuperSteel. We know every factor affecting its production. *Every* one!"

"Except the one that gave it the tensile strength it had," said Pete.

"Maybe you're right there," Cochran conceded, "but if that's true, it's a factor that can't be weighed, measured, or observed in any known manner. We couldn't produce another ounce of SuperSteel if our lives depended on it—except by accident."

"That last batch of tungsten—maybe it wouldn't hurt to add another tenth—" Thompson muttered lamely.

"No!" Willard snapped. "That's the one thing we must not do now—tinker with the charge and the alloy percentages. We've got to find out why we got SuperSteel with the formula we used or we won't find out anything!"

"I agree with that," said Cochran. "Let's stick to the routine that produced SuperSteel until we get some more. It's all we can do, outside of continued analysis of what we made to see why it's so tough."

"And my next ad was a doozy!" Roberts complained. "Now I guess I've got to kill it. What're we going to do with the orders we've accepted?"

"That's your problem," said Willard as he turned to the door. "You were so anxious to get them. Let's see you take care of them."

The whole thing was like one of those dreams where you cavort with houris on some south sea island all through the night, and then wake up to a morning of cold drizzle outside, a mouth like an old flannel jacket, and the wife gone home to Mother for two weeks.

It just hadn't happened. If there were not a few samples in the testing lab he would never believe that

SuperSteel had existed, Willard thought.

He was thinking that as he sat in the company cafeteria at noon. There was an executives' table where the gold badge boys were supposed to get priority service and quality, but Willard preferred to sit with the men from the mill. Somehow, the toughest cuts of meat, the wateriest soup, and the stalest bread seemed to find its way down the exec table. Willard felt in a mood to go back to the kitchen and find out just how that was managed.

His mood was interrupted by Dr. Lloyd Evans, the Director of Personnel and Counseling at Intermountain. Evans sat down and drew the menu toward him. "Too bad about this SuperSteel fluke," he said. "It would have been nice if you could have caught it before it played out. Have any idea why?"

"It's not supposed to be out yet," Willard said, suspiciously. "Where did you get it?"

"You pick things up around a place like this. They're hard to hide. Think you're going to find the answer?"

Willard shook his head. "We've checked on everything. We've measured the batches down to the last milligram. Temperatures to the hundredth of a degree. No variables. But no SuperSteel."

"How about personnel? Made any check on them?"

"What do you mean? The same crew's been with us all through the thing. Thompson, Manning, Hartley—"

"They're your foremen and crew chiefs. You know them, sure. But how about all the boys on the floor?"

Willard shrugged. "I don't know. They're all the same as far as I know. You think somebody new could have been hired and might be sabotaging the production? That's out! Such a thing would be impossible."

"Why don't you make a check, just for the heck of it?"

Willard hesitated over refusal of the ridiculous notion, then gave in and beckoned for a plug-in phone to be brought to the table. He called Personnel. "Get me any employment changes on the furnace crew and pouring floor during the past week."

"Better include the lab staff, too," Evans said.

In a moment Willard had the information. He hung up and put the phone aside. "Just as I told you. Nothing's changed. Only one man has left, John Ward, a craneman. And his place has been filled by moving up another employee. There's nobody new in contact with SuperSteel production—or, rather, lack of it."

"John Ward—" Evans said thoughtfully. "College boy, as I recall. Been working in steel every summer while going to school. Did Ward pour all the batches that came out as SuperSteel?"

"How the hell should I know that, either?"

"Find out."

Willard hesitated on the verge of refusal a second time, then reached for the phone with a patronizing gesture, as if to pamper a childish whim of his associate. This time he had to check the batch numbers of SuperSteel against the personnel working the various shifts at the time SuperSteel appeared. It took longer.

At last he hung up and looked across the table at Evans. "All right. Ward poured every batch of SuperSteel. Nobody else. But that doesn't prove a thing. A craneman couldn't affect the quality of a batch of steel even if he wanted to."

The psychologist smiled. "It's the only variable factor you've found so far. You don't have to take my advice, but I'd say that if you're smart you'll get Ward back here. Just to pour one batch for you, if nothing more."

"This is the first time I ever had lunch with a lunatic!"

The idea had a crazy, gnawing quality that wouldn't let go. Willard spent the afternoon personally supervising the charging of Number Two and Number Four. He reviewed the logs of previous charges, all the way back to the last time SuperSteel came from these furnaces. It was as Evans had said: Ward, the craneman, was the only variable he could find in the whole chain of factors.

At a couple minutes to five he called the personnel office again. "Miss Jensen—Willard of Test Lab—get me the file on John Ward who quit as craneman last week. Find out if he left a forwarding address."

While he waited, he reminded himself again that only an idiot would go this far, and that he wasn't going to carry it one step further.

"Mr. Ward left to attend classes at CalTech," said Miss Jensen. "I have his address in care of the school, if you want it."

As soon as he had written down the information, Willard wadded up the slip of paper and threw it in the nearest wastebasket. He walked out of the room feeling like a free man.

At ten o'clock that night he finally made telephone contact with John Ward at his dormitory address. The former craneman sounded wary, Willard thought.

"This is Mr. Willard, of Intermountain Steel," said the engineer. "I understand you were operating the crane on the pouring floor for us this summer."

"Yes."

"We've got a new man on the job, and there seems to be some trouble with the machinery. All our mechanics have had a look at it without finding anything wrong, but it still won't work right."

"I didn't have any trouble when I was running it," said Ward.

"That's what everyone tells me—that you could make it behave like a trained kitten. I know it sounds crazy, but we've tried everything else, and there might be some personal gimmick in the method of operation you used. It would be a great favor to us if you would come out and take over a shift, just to satisfy our feelings about this."

"I'm afraid there would be trouble if I did that," said Ward. "Mr. Masovitch told me he'd personally unhook my neck from my backbone if I ever set foot in the Intermountain plant again."

"Masovitch? The foreman?"

"Yes."

"Why?"

"He just didn't like the way I did some things."

"Then you didn't quit—you were fired?"

"I expected to work another quarter before coming back to school. But it's all right. I'm rather glad Mr. Masovitch fired me, now."

"Listen, don't worry about Masovitch. We want you to come back and help us out now. We'll pay all your expenses, including travel by plane, and will give you a hundred dollars for the shift. You can make it on the week-end when you're free of classwork. Better still, if you need to work some more, why don't you come on back until you're really ready to start school?"

"I couldn't do that. Everything is under way here now. But I can't very well turn down your special deal. I'll see you Sunday morning, if that's all right with you."

"I'll meet you at the airport!"

"Don't let Mr. Masovitch hear about this."

Willard was glad it was Sunday. He should have thought of that, himself. Few, if any, of the executive staff would be around. He might be able to get Ward in and out of the plant without anyone being particularly aware of his presence. He hoped so. He'd hate to have to explain to Cochran—or anyone else—why he was doing this.

He met the plane at a quarter to six Sunday morning, and picked up John Ward personally. He remembered seeing him around the plant, and liking his looks.

Ward was smiling as he stepped off the plane. "I'm sure I don't know what I can do for you, Mr. Willard. But it was a nice trip over."

"We'll see," said Willard, "We appreciate your coming. Nothing's lost, even if you aren't able to help us."

They got into Willard's car. "This sounds funny, I guess," he said. "Don't be afraid to say so, because we feel the same way about it. The only thing is, we've tried everything else except tearing down the whole machine."

There was a little wait, after they reached the plant and climbed to the crane cab. But Number One and Number Three were ready for tapping this morning. Ward tried the controls while they waited. "I don't see anything wrong," he said. "She's working just the same as when I left."

Willard nodded. "I don't know. Just go ahead and put her through her paces in your usual way."

He sat beside Ward through the morning hours as they watched the first white trickle of liquid fire burst from the furnaces and turn to a volcanic fury. He sensed the delicate touch of Ward's hands on the controls as the crane moved carefully above the bright hell below them. One by one the moulds filled, the color slowly dying in them.

"There's not a thing wrong with this crane," said Ward as he finished Number One. "You must have had a moron trying to run it."

"Jakes was handling her."

"That explains it. Get a man with some brains."

Ward finished the shift alone. Willard went back to his office and waited in solitude. He was aware for the first time that his hands were wet with sweat, and the back of his shirt was soaked. And it wasn't from the heat of the pouring floor. He was just plain jittery, wondering what those billets would turn out to be when they were cured, rolled, tempered, tested—

Ward thanked him for the check for pay and expenses when the shift was over. "I'll do that any week-end you like," he said, grinning. "But all you need to do is get that dope off the crane and she'll run all by herself."

Willard found it hard to sleep until samples of the batch could be tested. He forced himself to remain in his office the day they were tested. He got the results by phone.

Ward's batches were a long way from SuperSteel. They were slightly below normal, for the most part.

Evans looked up from his desk as Willard entered. "Well, it was a good idea, but it was a bust," the engineer said. "I got Ward here, as you suggested."

"I saw you driving in Sunday morning. The tests weren't any good?"

Willard shook his head with a smile. "You didn't really think they would be, did you? I guess I must have let myself get a little balmy, going for a proposition like that. Anyway, you can't say I haven't been willing to try everything." He turned to go.

"Wait a minute." Evans got up from behind his desk and came toward the engineer. "This should have worked. You haven't got any other variables, have you?"

"No. But we'll find some!"

"Any idea where to look?"

"No. But I know where we're *not* going to look—not any more."

"Tell me about Ward. Everything you noticed."

"Look—I've got work to do!"

"You haven't any other variables, remember."

In disgust, Willard recited everything he could remember about the young engineer-craneman, his looks, his manner, his attitude.

"You say Masovitch fired him?" Evans said wonderingly. "Can you imagine what for? Masovitch is a good steelman. If Ward is as good a craneman as you say, why did Masovitch fire him?"

"Who knows? And what difference does it make? Personal grudges come up without any rational foundation all the time. You personnel people know more about that than I do."

Evans nodded. "And from all you tell me there was absolutely no basis for Ward's firing. Why don't we go down and ask Masovitch himself?"

"I've got more important things to do!"

But Willard allowed himself to be led to the foreman's cubicle. The big Polish foreman was going over his production figures as Evans entered. "We just wanted to ask a few questions about one of the men who used to work for you," said the psychologist. "Fellow named John Ward."

Masovitch spat into the corner beyond his desk. "That nut? Why would anybody want to know anything about him?"

"You think he's a nut, huh? Why?"

"Because he is, that's why. Crazy as they come. One day he won't pour steel because the wind's blowing too hard outside. Next day he won't pour because it isn't blowing at all. Or maybe it's too hot, or too cold. Jeez, you'd think he had a little crystal ball up there in the cab, telling him what to do. He even started telling us how to tap the furnaces!"

Evans glanced at Willard. "He was a pretty crazy character, eh?" he said to the foreman. "When did you first notice this? Ever since he first came?"

"No—no, he was a nice kid at first. Wanted to do everything just right, just the way you told him. Then he went nuts all of a sudden, like I told you. You can't make steel with guys like that. You're going to look up some day and find 'em pouring a ladle full of hot metal down the back of your neck!"

"Was this about the time that SuperSteel began to be produced?"

Masovitch looked thoughtful, as if going back in time to that remarkable event. "About then, I guess," he said matter-of-factly. "Right about that time. Say, when are we going to get some more batches like that? That was real great stuff!"

Evans walked back along the corridor that took Willard to his test lab. Neither spoke until they reached the doorway to Willard's office.

"You'd better get Ward back here," Evans said finally. "Get him to do exactly and whatever crazy thing he was doing when SuperSteel came out. You'll never sleep easy until you do."

"Now you're trying to tell me a nut was responsible for SuperSteel!"

"Ward didn't look like a nut to you, did he? I thought you said he was quite a serious young student."

"He appeared that way."

"You ever hear of a man named Stradivarius?" said Evans slowly.

"The fiddle maker?"

"The same," said Evans. "For about a century and a half, people have been trying to make violins as good as Stradivarious made them. Nobody has done it yet."

"Now wait a minute—"

"The varnish has been analyzed, the wood has been identified, the measurements have been taken. Everything that could possibly have gone into the making of Stradivarius violins has been measured, weighed and duplicated as near as is physically possible. But they just don't play the same."

"What are you trying to tell me?" Willard felt an unaccountable anger rising.

"Just what made a Strad violin so good that it can't be duplicated after all these years of trying?"

"How in hell should I know? You just said everything's been analyzed without finding out."

"And that's all anybody can say. But suppose Stradivarious just *wanted* his violins to be better than any other violins ever made."

"He'd have to do a lot more than just want—"

"Suppose somebody—John Ward, say — just *wanted* the steel he worked on to be the best ever made—"

"You're absolutely and completely off your rocker. Why don't you go see a head shrinker?" said Willard quietly.

The two men let their eyes lock without speaking for a full thirty seconds. Then Evans resumed slowly. "John Ward knows how to make SuperSteel. He doesn't *know* that he knows, but he does."

"He doesn't *do* anything to it!"

"Yes, he does. He pours it from a furnace ladle into a mould. He's a part of the production process, and while playing that small part he gets into the batch that ingredient that makes a steel such as the world has never seen. Don't you want to know how he does it?"

"But if *he* doesn't even know—"

Evans nodded. "That's the catch. Stradivarius didn't know how he produced his wonderful violins, either. He never taught anybody else how to do it. Did you ever watch one of these computing geniuses at work? I saw a Swiss farm girl once who could multiply twenty digit numbers in thirty seconds flat. She could recite everything she'd ever read, word for word. Otherwise, she was a dolt."

"John Ward's no dolt."

"That's where we're lucky. He may be capable of the kind of introspection that will reveal how he does it. Or the talent may sink completely out of sight the moment he realizes he has it."

"We don't even know if he has it!"

"Get him back here. Permanently. We'll put every kind of test on him we can think of until he becomes suspicious. We won't tell him what's up until he does. Then we'll tell, and see what happens to his ability.

"Maybe he won't even believe it."

"That, in itself, may be enough to wipe it out."

Willard moved along slowly to a corridor window that looked out on the plant's great coke ovens. "I'm afraid I'm the one that's never going to believe this thing, no matter what evidence I'm shown. How *could* it be possible?"

There was still a major problem that remained unsolved, Willard realized as he left Evans. Money. He went directly to the office of the President. He strode past Dorothy, the receptionist Cochran had hired chiefly as artwork.

"The Boss in?" Willard said.

"No appointments this afternoon, Mr. Willard. Mr. Cochran gave me strict instructions. Mr. Willard—!"

He was already in. Cochran frowned in the middle of a phone conversation with someone in New York. The engineer looked out the window until he heard the phone replaced.

"You've always said you believe in letting a man do his job in his own way," he said.

Cochran hesitated warily. "That's the philosophy I've tried to follow from this office. What's on your mind, Willard?"

"A hundred thousand dollars for a special project I think will be worth it."

"You're not talking peanuts, even for these days of reputed excess profits. What the hell do you want a hundred grand for?"

"That has to be my secret."

"Isn't that letting the crust rise pretty thick? I have to account for the way I run this plant."

"You wouldn't authorize it if you knew what I wanted it for."

"SuperSteel?"

"Yes."

"You think it'll solve the problem?"

"No—not really."

"Then what—?"

"It's something that's got to be tried. Something *I've* got to try before we say it can't be done. That's all I'm going to say about it."

Cochran frowned irritably. "It's going to be a red-letter day when I finally find a good enough excuse to fire you. Go ahead, set up your project file. The money'll be allotted. But I expect to see a hundred thousand dollars worth of results!"

Willard reached John Ward by phone again late that night. The former craneman recognized his voice at once.

"Hello, Mr. Willard," he said happily. "You need me for any more hundred dollar shifts on the crane?"

"Yes, as a matter of fact, quite a few."

"I'm sorry, I was only kidding."

"I wasn't," said Willard. "How would you like to come back and work for Intermountain on a steady job for a year, Ward?"

"I'm afraid I couldn't do that. I intend to finish school and then go into metallurgical engineering."

"You didn't ask about the salary. We'd pay you enough so that you could finish school without worrying about part time and summer work."

"How much?"

"Fifty thousand dollars."

"For one year?"

"We'll sign a contract on it."

There was a long period of silence at the other end. Finally, Ward came back. "You want me to work just as a craneman?"

"Most of the time. There might be a chance to do a little lab work on occasion, but it would be mostly on the crane."

"I don't know, Mr. Willard," Ward said. "It's like asking me to sell a piece of my life. It's a question whether the price is worth it in terms of what I want to do."

"We'll make it seventy-five thousand dollars, Ward. What is it that you want to do?"

"I want to be a scientist. I want to know everything there is to know about metals—why they hold together, why some are strong and some are weak, why some conduct electricity and some resist it. I want to know their molecules as well as if I could see them, and put them together, like blocks, in any shape and form and strength I choose."

And perhaps you already can, Willard thought soberly. *Why do you think you must go to school to learn those things?*

"We'd like to help you realize those ambitions and dreams," he said aloud. "Money isn't everything, but it sure helps a lot."

"I don't understand why you're willing to pay me this. There's something important you haven't told me."

"I'm reserving the right to withhold that information until the end of the year. I can guarantee it's honorable and honest, but I can't tell you what it is."

"You make it sound very mysterious."

"You'll be asked to do nothing for Intermountain that you have not done before."

"Let me sleep on it."

"We know about Mr. Masovitch," said Willard slowly. "He told us why he fired you. You won't have any more trouble with him. You can proceed just as before. If the wind isn't right, you can wait until it is. If it's too cold, you can wait until the sun comes up farther."

He heard Ward's breath suck sharply at the other end of the line. The man's voice was filled with quiet excitement when he spoke again.

"I'll be there day after tomorrow," he said.

The production of SuperSteel resumed with the first batch he poured.

"How is he?" Evans asked. "Does this present setup seem to affect his attitude or the quality of the steel?"

"The first batch he poured ran only seventy-eight thousand p.s.i. above normal, but everything since then has gone over eighty, where it used to be."

"He knows what he's doing," said Evans. "He knows why we brought him back."

"You think so?"

"He'd be an idiot not to recognize it. Why do you think he does all those crazy tricks of timing his pours and adjusting to the weather?"

Willard shook his head. "Eccentric. Or crazy, I guess. Whatever you want to call it. But as long as it doesn't hurt the steel, I guess we can put up with it. Production goes down when he wants to wait, but we can afford that for the amount of SuperSteel we're getting."

"Did it ever occur to you that maybe *that* is the way he makes SuperSteel?"

"By waiting on the weather? By timing his pour according to that weird formula he uses?"

"Yes."

"I guess I'm willing to listen to anything," said Willard sadly. "I never believed Ward had anything to do with it in the first place. Now, all I care about is learning *how*. If you say his shenanigans are responsible, I'm willing to be shown."

"It's not that easy." Evans shook his head. "That's the part I don't think Ward understands himself. He's just shooting in the dark, but he's hitting pretty close!"

"Someday I'm going to wake up and discover this was all a beautiful nightmare!"

Evans growled irritably at Willard's persistent refusal to accept the obvious. "Does Cochran know about Ward yet?"

Willard shook his head. "I don't think he's noticed. I've told Ward nobody is to know about the deal except you and me. I don't know how long he'll hold still for that kind of treatment, but he's signed the contract. What do we do if we can't tell him why he's here—or that we know he knows already?"

Evans smiled. "We don't want to play ostrich indefinitely. I just want a substantial period in which to observe him as he now functions, without disturbing him by obvious study."

"It's out of my hand now," said Willard, rising. "We've applied every test and measurement we know in order to find out what goes into this steel. We don't know any more than when we started. It's up to you to pull it out of Ward. If you need help by way of a staff, we can still get something in the budget."

"I may need plenty before this is over!"

President Cochran was pleased enough that SuperSteel production had resumed, but its previous decline had taught him they were on shaky ground. He vetoed a resumption of the massive trade campaign that Roberts wanted to get under way again.

He stood with Willard and Roberts overlooking the pouring floor while the sales chief protested they were losing the opportunity of a lifetime.

"We're not going to get caught in the kind of jam we had before," Cochran said. "We'll fill some of the back orders that weren't taken care of, and let it be known by word of mouth that we have small amounts available to our old customers. That will take care of all we can turn out until we find out the how of this thing."

"We could put in more furnace capacity. Double production!" Roberts protested.

"When we learn *how* to make SuperSteel," Cochran said with finality. Then he pointed down to the crane, moving slowly beyond them. "We've got a new man there. I hadn't noticed the change before. I wonder when he came on.

"Seems to be a good operator," Willard mumbled. "Let's go down and have a look at the charge logs," he added quickly, drawing at Cochran's arm.

"It's that kid that was here once before," Roberts said. "Thought he left to go to school or something. Must not have panned out. These guys care more for money than education these days. He's likely to regret it ten years from now. What's running a crane compared with a good education?"

While Evans studied Ward physically and psychologically like a white rat running a maze, Willard set up an observation crew that watched every move he made, by telescope and by hidden instruments in the crane cab. Ward had agreed to the physical tests as a condition of employment. He made no protest when these sometimes included an electroencephalograph reading, though he looked inquiringly at the nurses and doctors who examined him.

As far as Willard knew, however, the craneman didn't know about the observation of his working habits and techniques. At the end of two months the test engineer believed he knew everything that Ward did in producing SuperSteel.

One night, on a graveyard shift when Ward was home asleep, Willard took the crane controls himself. Carefully, and with meticulous attention to the fantastic detail Ward had accumulated, he poured a batch.

There wasn't a molecule of SuperSteel in the lot.

Willard began to wonder if, somehow, they were all being taken for one big ride. SuperSteel–its appearance only when Ward was around—the apparently psychic relationship between the craneman and the new metal–the impossibility of duplicating it when Ward was absent–

On the face of it, the whole thing looked as if some fantastic hoax were being perpetrated. Only the tension gauges in his own laboratory kept Willard from this conclusion.

The day after Willard's failure to duplicate the young craneman's effort he decided to quit beating around the bush, Evans or no Evans. He called Ward to his office before the shift began.

Ward acted as if he had been expecting something. He twisted his workman's gloves uneasily. Willard came to the point.

"You know about SuperSteel," he said.

Ward nodded; his nervous fiddling with the gloves increased.

"We think you have something to do with it."

Ward nodded again. "I know," he said.

"What do you know?" Willard demanded. "You know we suspect this? Or you know how SuperSteel is made?"

"Both," said Ward.

"I'll skip asking why you haven't said anything about it before now. But you did agree to sign a contract, and you signed a patent agreement also. You do have a certain obligation to disclose any such information to the company."

"I'm more than willing," Ward said. "I've been trying for weeks to figure out how to do it. There's no one here to whom I could teach it."

"Tell me. No–wait. I want Evans and Cochran to hear this."

The test engineer disappeared, returning in fifteen minutes with the psychologist and Intermountain's president. They sat at the small conference table in Willard's office as Ward looked uncomfortably from one to the other.

"Now," said Willard.

"I don't know how to say it," Ward said in obvious misery. "When you made your offer I told myself I was going to let you have the secret as soon as possible–but I don't know how to do it."

"Just describe what you know of making SuperSteel," said Cochran. "Let us judge whether we can learn it or not." His voice sounded as if the long tension within himself could not be held much longer.

"There are so many things that count," said Ward, musingly. "Masovitch thought I was crazy because I was concerned with temperature out-doors, and with barometric pressure, and humidity. All those things count. But there's more, too. The feel of the lessening weight in the ladle as you pour. The thickness of the falling column. The height from which it's dropped. And these things aren't the same all the time. They vary with the constituency of the batch. You have to know how to feel just what's inside the ladle in order to know how to get the best steel out of it. Do you see what I mean?"

The others stared at him. Finally, Evans broke the silence. "The Strad Effect," he said slowly.

"What are you talking about?" Cochran demanded angrily.

Evans told him what he'd said previously to Willard about the violin-maker. "You can say that any man whose skill goes beyond the normal through an almost psychic understanding of his materials is operating under the Stradivarius Effect. You physicists like names like that." He smiled in Willard's direction. "I should think you'd find it appropriate."

"Quite appropriate," said Willard. "But whatever you call it, we've got to find a way to duplicate it."

"There's more to it than you've understood," said Ward. "When a man loves a thing he develops that understanding of materials. The love for the skill comes first."

Evans nodded. "That's understandable."

"That's why I can't teach it!" said Ward.

The others looked at one another in silence again. "You mean to say I don't love this business enough to be able to make the best steel?" Cochran said.

"No," said Ward.

"You're crazy! There's nothing I wouldn't do to put this little outfit on top of the heap! I'd get down there on the pouring floor in overalls two shifts a day, myself, if I thought it would yield Super-Steel!"

"That's just it," said Ward. "You love the company, the business end of steel-making. You want Intermountain to be the biggest of its kind, and give your own personal pride in the management of it.

"But you don't love steel."

Cochran's face darkened. "Why, you—"

"Take it easy," Evans said. "The man's telling the truth, and you know it. I'm just beginning to see what this is all about. How many steelmen in the whole country care for steel the way Stradivarius cared for violin making?"

He smiled as the others failed to answer. "Take Masovitch," he continued. "What does he care for?

He's the foreman, but any other job would be just as good as long as it gave him three squares and let him feed his kids right. You, Willard—how much are you in love with steel?"

"I don't see what that's got to do with anything!" the test engineer snapped, almost irritably. "I'm not a steel fanatic, certainly, but I'd like to see the job done right. I'd like to see SuperSteel put on a production basis for the sheer satisfaction of doing it. I don't see why I can't learn the technique as well as anybody else."

"You're closer than any, maybe," said Ward. "But there are so many variables in every batch. You have to know what to do about each one. The rules are no good. You have to feel how to do the right thing at the right time to make the steel good. You can't feel it unless you care enough. Stradivarius cared enough about violins so that he could make them all nearly perfect, even though no two pieces of wood were ever alike. That's the way it has to be with steel."

A wall had risen between them. On one side, Evans and the steelmakers seemed to watch Ward through a thickening barrier they could not penetrate. Ward, doubtless, felt the same on his side of the table.

"I guess you won't need me around here any more," he said. "I know you hired me and offered me all that money so you could learn how to make SuperSteel. I can't teach you. I'm sorry."

"What do you mean, we won't need you?" Cochran demanded. "You don't need to go back to school to learn about metals! You know more than all the metallurgists in the world, put together. I'll double your salary if you'll keep on producing SuperSteel for us."

"You can hardly expect a man of his intellect to continue as a craneman," said Evans. "He belongs in a university laboratory."

Ward smiled.

"I won't be a craneman," he said, "any more than Stradivarius was a wood carver. If you really want me, nothing in the world could tear me away from steelmaking. And I'll make it better and better —every batch I pour!"

From the gallery they watched him go back to the cab of the crane. Cochran shook his head disbelievingly. "Stradivarius! Who'd ever expect to find him in a steel mill!"

Then he turned suddenly and strode off.

"Where are you going in such a hurry?" Evans called.

"To get my overalls," Cochran called back. "I'm going to make a liar out of Stradivarius!"

WONDERS ARE MANY

by

L. Sprague de Camp

THIS SECTION WILL, *deo volente,* be a regular feature of this magazine. It will consist of articles and fillers on factual matters of interest to readers of imaginative fiction. It will deal with curious, controversial, and speculative aspects of science, invention, history, mythology, pseudo-science, supernaturalism, and imaginative fiction.

If anybody has a subject he would like discussed, let him write me care of the magazine. I will not promise to comply with all requests, as some topics would be less fascinating to most readers than to the persons proposing them, and there are some about which nobody knows enough to say aught. But I shall be glad of suggestions.

The title of this feature-column is from Sophokles' *Antigone.* The passage continues:

Wonders are there many—none more wonderful than man./His the might that crosses seas swept white by storm winds . . .

—(Hamilton translation.)

So, let us begin with a discussion of our future.

OUR BIOLOGICAL FUTURE — I

In a well-known science-fiction story,* the hero goes three million years into the future. At that point on the time-track, he finds that man has dwindled to thirty-five super-geniuses whose skinny little bodies cannot hold up their enormous heads without props. All they do is sit and think. Horrified, the hero massacres the lot and returns to his own time, excitedly boasting of killing off this race of "monsters."

Other writers have caused man to mutate into a superman, a telepath, or (after an atomic war) a freak with three eyes or two heads. Every time one of my colleagues broods on the hydrogen-bomb menace, he writes a story wherein man has been changed by hard radiations into something halfway between a human being and an emu, an aard-vark, or an octopus.

What is really likely to happen? In recent years, the sciences of genetics and evolution-theory have made such giant strides that we can now form quite a clear idea of how we got this way and what is now befalling us.

In the last two million years, we evolved from small, erect, ground-living man-apes like those found fossil in Africa. Contrary to what was once thought, the bodies of these Australopithecines had become quite human-looking at a time when their heads were still for practical purposes those of anthropoid apes.

During most of this time, our forebears were tiny isolated bands of hunters. Three forces caused them to evolve. These were mutation, selection, and genetic drift.

Mutation is a sudden change in the mechanism of heredity. As you may know, nearly all the machinery of heredity dwells in the chromosomes. These are thread-like particles in the cells of living things. Different species have different patterns of chromosomes. The chromosomes are made of hundreds of particles, called genes, strung together. Each gene is thought to be a giant molecule of protein, like a tame plant virus.

A human sperm or ovum has twenty-four chromosomes. The

*Harry Bates: "Alas, All Thinking!" (*Astounding Science-Fiction, June*, 1935; reprinted in *The Other Worlds* and *Imagination Unlimited*).

L. SPRAGUE DE CAMP, one of the most prolific writers in science fiction, is also one of the most scholarly. Here he explores odd by-paths in the history of knowledge, and occasionally will review non-fiction books of interest to s-f readers — both exclusively for VANGUARD. *He is the author of a historical novel, "An Elephant for Aristotle", just published by Doubleday.*

number of genes in a complete set of these chromosomes is estimated at ten-to-twenty thousand. At conception, a sperm joins an ovum, adding its twenty-four chromosomes to those of the ovum. This makes forty-eight chromosomes in the embryonic cell, with twenty-to-forty thousand genes. Then, when the cell starts to grow, it divides into two. At this time the chromosomes go through a kind of ritual-dance, which ends with each chromosome splitting lengthwise into two. They have been making duplicates of themselves out of the chemicals in the cell. One set of forty-eight chromosomes goes into one of the new cells and the rest into the other.

Every time a cell divides, this division happens again, until the grown organism comes to create sex-cells for reproductive purposes. Then the chromosomes separate once without splitting, so that each sex-cell gets only twenty-four. The 24-chromosome sex-cell is called a *gamete* and the 48-chromosome body-cell a *zygote*.

As you see, every zygote has a duplicate set of chromosomes. If we give them Roman numbers, there are two I's, two II's, and so on up to the two XXIV's. If we number the genes on each chromosome, each No. I will begin with numbers 1, 2, and so on.

The two I-1 genes of a given zygote are much alike; so are the two I-2's, the two VI-437's, and the two XX-986's. Often they are identical, in which case the organism is called a *homozygote* with regard to that gene, whichever it be.

However, the two genes of a gene-pair may differ. In fact, there may be a number of alternative patterns of gene that can equally well occupy a given gene-site, say the I-1 spot on either No. 1 chromosome, just as you might have any of several different makes of tire on the left front wheel of your car. These different gene-types that occupy a given site in the chromosomes are called the *alleles* of the gene. When different alleles of a gene occupy the two I-1 places, the organism is call a *heterozygote* as regards that gene.

Of each such pair of genes, you get one from each parent. Each of your children will get one gene like one member of each pair you have, but it is a matter of luck which one he will get.

Genes carry particular traits. That is, each gene affects the growth of at least one part of your body and decides its size, shape, color, or other quality. Many genes affect several parts each, while many characters like the color of your skin are the result of many genes, scattered among the chromosomes, acting together. Such a group of genes that work in concert is called a *polygene*. An organ controlled by a polygene is not inherited according to Mendel's simple ratios but follows more complex formulas. The growth of the human brain is governed by a large polygene, so that genius in men does not follow any simple one-two-one ratio, like that which obtains with eye-color in men or height in sweet peas.

Thus you are a mosaic of characters that have come down from thousands of ancestors. And now for mutations.

Mutations were called "sports" by animal-breeders long before scientists studied them. The first mutation definitely recorded was a short-legged lamb, born in 1791 into a flock owned by Seth Wright of Massachusetts.

In the 1890's, the Dutch botanist Hugo de Vries recognized mutations as part of the mechanism of evolution. De Vries supposed that all mutations were big sudden changes that made a new species all at once. He thought this because he actually found such a drastic change in the evening primrose, *Oenothera*. In fact, however, this was a special kind of mutation called *polyploidy*: doubling the number of chromosomes. It is fairly common in plants but extremely rare in animals. When animal polyploids occur, they usually leave no descendants because their offspring are sexually abnormal.

The kind of mutation that often occurs in animals is the gene-mutation or point-mutation. Although genes can be passed on down for thousands of generations unchanged, once in a while an accident betides one. Some atoms are knocked off or twisted askew, or an extra atom is added, or the gene's position in the chromosome is changed, or the gene is duplicated or lost. If such a change occurs in a gamete, and the new gene-pattern is passed on to an offspring, the offspring will have some new character that none of its ancestors had. The same gene can change in many different ways.

One gene in a gamete does not have much chance of mutating. However, with ten to twenty thousand genes in a sex-cell, mutation is not rare. Some geneticists think the human gamete has about one chance in four of mutating during its short life. Since you get one gamete from each parent, you have twice the chance of getting a mutation from two parents as from one. In other words, you have an almost even chance of being a mutant—that is, of differing from your parents by a mutation. As each of them had the same chance of being a mutant in their turn, your chance of differing from your grandparents by one or more mutations is higher yet—between four-fifths and seven-eighths—and so on back. For practical purposes, *we are all mutants.*

Then why don't we all have two heads? Because most mutations are small—so small we can hardly detect them. In fact, many mutations may go on all the time with such small effects that we don't even know about them. They may make your digestion work a little better or worse, or your eyesight a little keener or dimmer, or your arteries harden a little sooner or later.

In point of fact, most mutations we know about are harmful or destructive. They make your eyes and digestion and arteries worse, not better. Constructive mutations cannot be more than a fraction of 1% of the total. The bigger the mutation, the smaller its chance of being good. Most drastic mutations are lethal. They kill off the organism in embryo or in infancy.

The reason for this is simple. A gene is an enormously complex little bit of biochemical machinery, exquisitely adapted to its task of controlling the growth of some part or parts of the body, either by itself or in coöperation with other genes. To expect a big random mutation to better it is like trying to improve a watch by hitting it with a hammer.

Even if the lethal mutations be barred from consideration, nevertheless, if all non-lethal mutants are given an equal chance of survival and reproduction, the overall effect of mutation is overwhelmingly harmful to the species, because the great majority of mutations are destructive.

While the number of possible mutations is enormous, and any gene may mutate in many ways, some genes mutate more than others, and many undergo certain mutations over and over. Geneticists estimate that the mutation causing chondrodystrophic dwarfism (fetal rickets) occurs about once in every 10,000 human births, and that one responsible for hemophilia about once in 50,000. The hemophilia that Queen Victoria passed on to her descendants in the Russian and Spanish royal families was probably such a mutation.

Although rare, constructive or beneficial mutations happen, too. That is how evolution takes place. In a wild state, living things with destructive mutations tend to die young, while those with constructives have more than their share of offspring and take the place of those without them. Thus, in Europe, the black mutation of several moths has become beneficial around sooty cities because moths that have it are harder for hungry birds to see. Therefore these black moths have taken the place of the normal speckled races. Since men have been using antibiotic drugs on bacteria and new insecticides on insects, many species of bacteria and insects have developed strains immune to these poisons.

We know some but not all of the causes of mutations. Hard radiations bring on some; not only those from man-made things like X-ray machines and atomic bombs, but also from the slight but ever-present radioactivity of the air, from cosmic rays, and the earth, from radioactive minerals. Dosing animals like vinegar-flies with X-rays greatly speeds up their rate of mutation.

As far as evolution is concerned, though, the slow action of the weak natural radioactivity, acting over the centuries, causes far more mutations than the violent radiations from atomic explosions acting over a short time only. It has been estimated that if atomic tests keep on at their present rate for a century, the mutation-rate of men might be raised by one and a half to three percent. Most of the monsters would die young as they do now, while no one mutation will make a superman. It will not even make a genius, because the growth of the brain is governed by a large polygene, and it takes the right alleles of all the genes of the polygene acting at once to make a genius. Genius is therefore a highly unpredictable event.

An atomic war would of course dose many more people at one time with radiations. But such a war would not likely last long. Therefore its long-term genetic effect would be much less than some have feared. Civilization stands to suffer far more in such a war from the annihilation of cities and the resulting breakdown of systems and institutions than from the rise in the mutation-rate of the survivors. Careless use of X-rays by people like shoe-salesmen may present as big a hazard to our heredity as bombs.

Besides radiations, some chemicals affect the mutation-rate in some organisms. Mustard gas, some peroxides, and ethyl sulfate raise it, at least in experimental animals. So does formaldehyde, which automobile-exhausts spew forth. So do the purine bases, a group of chemicals, including caffein, related to uric acid. Therefore it is not impossible that drinking tea and coffee increases mutations in men. Sudden changes in temperature speed mutations in insects but are less likely to affect large animals like us because our gametes are better protected.

An agency that promotes mutations is called a *mutagen*. Recently it has been found that there are *antimutagens* as well, which lower the rate of mutation. A small class of chemicals called ribosides have this effect on bacteria. Whether there are antimutagens for higher forms of life is not yet known.

How bad is it to raise the mutation-rate? Without some mutations we could never have evolved from lizards, and without them the breed of men could not be much improved in the future.

The extra mutations caused by the mutagens of civilization are of exactly the same kind as those that have been happening for billions of years. The effect of these mutagens is to cause more mutations, but not mutations of a different kind. So we shall not get a race of two-headed men, bombs or no bombs.

However, some geneticists think that *all* mutations caused by hard radiations are destructives. They think the impact of such rays on the genes is too violent, too much like hitting a watch with a hammer, to improve them.

Moreover, many serious defects, like mongolian idiocy and cleft palate, may not be due to mutations. They may be caused, instead, by accidental damage to the growing embryo.

Nonetheless, there is still a sinister side to mutations. Among wild animals and primitive men, destructives are always arising and then being destroyed by the secondary great evolutionary force: *selection.*

This is the "survival of the fittest" of which Darwin's follower Spencer wrote. The expression does not mean that the fittest necessarily had to prove his fitness by walloping his fellow-caveman over the head. It merely means that he had to be enough stronger, healthier, smarter, brisker, and more fertile so that on the average he would leave more descendants.

Some common human traits that do not fit very well into civilized life can be explained on the ground that they helped those who had them to survive as hunters. For instance, reading that daily chronicle of the crimes and follies of mankind known as a newspaper, you may wonder at the bent of men to divide into factions along any convenient line of demarcation—racial, religious, linguistic, cultural, political, or merely sentimental—and fight it out with implacable hatred and bloodthirsty ferocity.

But, in a hunting-band, this factiousness has its use. Such a band has its optimum size. Under typical hunting-culture conditions, this size is about forty to eighty people, of whom ten to twenty are adult males.

At any one time, the area that the hunters can cover is limited by the distance they can hike away from their camp, kill their game, and drag it back to camp in a couple of days. If the size of the band much exceeds the optimum, there are more mouths to feed, but the hunters cannot hunt a larger area. They can only hunt the same area more intensely, whereupon the game is killed off or flees the neighborhood, and the band starves. Therefore it is to the hunters' advantage that, when the band exceeds a certain size, factions shall arise, and the quarrels among them shall force the band to split up. This is a speculation, but a reasonable one from what we know.

Again, people of the intellectual type have, from time immemorial, bemoaned the fact that they were such a small minority, lost in a sea of brainless buffoons and ignorant ruffians. But, while a few intellectuals are useful to the hunting-band for shamans and bards, a band made up entirely of intellectuals would probably perish, because these deep thinkers would be speculating on the origin of the cosmos or inventing the bicycle when they should be keeping their minds on spearing that salmon.

In a wild state, then, the species is kept hale and whole and betimes even bettered by the interaction of mutation and selection. Destructive mutations are always arising but are likewise being destroyed by selection. Often, however, they are not gotten rid of right away, because most mutations are *recessives.* This means that both genes of a gene-pair must belong to the mutated allele of the gene before the effects of the mutation become apparent.

Therefore, living things that carry the mutation as a recessive trait suffer from it little or not at all but can still pass it on. If the mutation is one that happens again and again, the number of heterozygotes rises until there are so many that they sometimes mate with one another instead of with the unmutated majority. When this happens, a fraction of their offspring are homozygotes displaying the mutation. If it be a destructive, they tend to die sooner than others of their species. Thus the species reaches a balance between the rate of mutation and the rate of elimination.

Sometimes a state of things called *balanced polymorphism* comes to pass. This is when a heterozygote is more viable than either of the two kinds of homozygote: the one with the mutation and the one without. For instance, in some malarial parts of Africa, people have a high proportion of the recessive gene-allele causing sickle-cell anemia in homozygotes. The heterozygotes (with one anemia-making gene) resist falciparum malaria better than those without this allele at all. So, while selection weeds out the homozygotes of this mutation, it tends to preserve the heterozygotes. And these bring forth more anemic homozygotes.

Thus mutations put constant pressure on a species, blurring its genetic design. A common type of mutation deprives the creature of an organ or a function. The loss of a gene is likely to have this effect. If the organ is not needed, the mutation happens again and again until the type without the organ becomes the normal one.

This is the process of *rudimentation,* which results in eyeless cave-creatures and those hairless primates called men. At some stage in their evolution, our ancestors dwelt in tropical forests where hair was not needed for warmth, so the hairless mutation got rid of it everywhere, save in a few spots where it protected tender tissues against sunburn or insect-bites.

Thus any organ or function not protected by selection is apt to be lost. Moreover, if the genes that built the organ disappear completely, the organ probably cannot be regained. Mutations do sometimes occur in reverse—that is, canceling a previous mutation—but this is rare. Our forebears failed to re-grow their pelts on moving to colder climes and had to invent clothes instead.

Contrariwise, if an animal has a prominent organ, the organ is probably useful even if we do not know just how it is used. It once was thought, for example, that the woolly mammoth's tusks were useless, since they were so long and curly that they crossed at the tips and so were no good for fighting or digging. Now it has been guessed that they were used as snow-shovels to get at food in winter.

When the pressure of selection relaxes, as it has with mankind, many destructive mutations spread through the species because those who get them are not eliminated. Every advance in medicine enables more people with defects to live and breed like everyone else.

In other words, every species is subject to constant degenerative *mutation-pressure*. In the wild state, this is counterbalanced by selection; but civilization, by mitigating the rigor of selection, allows mutation-pressure to work its effects almost unchecked. It might mean something that color-blindness is only about one percent in Eskimos, New Guineans, and Navahos, but around seven or eight percent among the long-civilized Chinese, Europeans, and white Americans.

The remaining evolutionary force is *genetic drift*. This is the random variation of small inbreeding groups away from the original type. It comes about partly through mutations and partly as a result of the chance loss of types without regard to their adaptive value. In a large interbreeding population, different alleles of the various genes occur in various proportions. These ratios will stay about the same indefinitely unless changed by selection.

Suppose, however, that neither brown eyes nor blue eyes have any advantage over the other, which is probably true. Then a large population in which, say, one-tenth of the people have the gene that makes blue eyes, will keep this proportion for ages. But, if the group is only twenty human beings, two with blue-eye genes, an accident can easily rid the group of the blue-eye gene for good. Some odd and apparently useless racial traits of small, long-isolated populations, like the high percentage of Rh-negative blood in the Basques, may be the result of genetic drift.

[*This is the first in a series of articles on our biological future.*]

"To produce a mighty book, you must choose a mighty theme. No great and enduring volume can ever be written on the flea, though many there be that have tried it." —Herman Melville.

THE TALES THEY TELL

by

Lester del Rey

NO BOOK WAS EVER SO BAD THAT someone didn't like it, if only the author; and probably no book ever escaped someone's intense dislike. Subjective reactions cannot be fully removed from judging a book, and inevitably my own personal reactions are going to color my evaluations.

Yet there are certain fixed values in writing of any kind; a novel is a matter of craft as well as art, and every craft has objective rules we can use to judge it. Otherwise there would be no need for editors, nor any way for them to separate good from bad. Even art in the final analysis must meet these tests of craftsmanship. And since my reviews will be based on such rules, let's look at the major ones I'll use as my guides.

First, as the quotation from Melville indicates, a novel must have something to say about a subject of enough importance to the reader to be of interest. This theme should operate through a plot, which is simply a meaningful pattern of action and reaction. Naturally, the plot must revolve around characters who are credible and sufficiently vital for the reader to care what happens to them, and their actions should seem to belong to them, not to be caused by the author's need to keep the plot going somehow. There must be some emotional intensity and enough inventiveness to avoid trite situations tritely strung together. There should be enough honesty to avoid phoney problems that could be solved if the characters stopped acting like idiots, or solutions that involve last-minute miracles or cavalry charges over the hill. We'd like a little color and background to keep the action from seeming to occur on a bare stage. Stylistically, the writing should be skillful enough to avoid annoying us, at a minimum.

These are all elementary rules, but they become doubly important in any field of fantasy, because we're dealing with something basically incredible; we need every trick in the book to make things believable. And for our own specialized form of the novel, we have other peculiar rules of our own.

One of the strongest is that science fiction must involve science! I have no absolute rule about how much science is wise; I think the balance between science and fiction must be determined by the novel itself, and the only safe rule is that the story should be one that couldn't happen without the science and extrapolation from science in it. Once the science is there, however, it must be honest science or honest extrapolation from real science, and the story must stick to the basic postulates it sets up. The same rules apply to fantasy or science-fantasy, except that any postulates can be used, provided they are used ingeniously and consistently. Finally, the most should be made of any postulate used; if we are dealing with a world having immortality, I'd like to see how that affects the economy, religion, construction of cars, marriage relationships, etc.; a good novel must make the most of what it uses.

Having stated what I consider the duties of a writer, maybe I'd better outline what I think my own duties here are. I'm not interested in summarizing novels so that lazy people can discuss them without reading. I'd like to be able to "improve the breed" by critical evaluation, but I'm extremely doubtful of my own talents along this line; I feel that many critics are called but few are proven. So all I can do is to review what the publishers bring out in the hope that I'll make it easier for other readers to spend their money wisely for books they'll enjoy. That is optimistic enough a goal, without going further.

I also want to keep this column as close to book publication dates as possible, hereafter. This time, however, there was too little time to alert publishers and get advance copies; I hope that the books under discussion will still be on sale when you read this. And now, to turn to them . . .

NO BLADE OF GRASS, by John Christopher. Simon & Schuster, New York. 218pp. $2.95.

Probably more people will read

or see this story than any other by a science fiction writer, which may or may not help the field, but which makes this an important novel. Movie rights have already been sold for a very handsome figure, and it was originally serialized in *The Saturday Evening Post,* where it received an unprecedented full-page build-up as the story that shocked the editors. It was not labelled as science fiction, however.

Actually, this is what I'd call marginal *science* fiction. It uses one of the best basic postulates I've seen, and I'm kicking myself for not having thought of it; while not 100% new, no real use was made of this idea before. It begins with a virus that suddenly appears and runs wild, destroying all members of the grass family—grass, rice, wheat, etc. At one blow, the cereals and fodder for meat animals are wiped out, making starvation inevitable for most of humanity within a brief time. We then follow a small group of people—from London through a world of desperate brutality toward an isolated valley where they believe life can be maintained—and from civilization to the mores of the primitive tribe.

On the science level, the development of the virus and the futile fight against it are well thought out; but once the world doom is established, no more is done with the idea. It is only a device to make the story possible, and it's dismissed when its work is done. We see little of what happens to animals and pets. We rarely get even adequate detail on the changing landscape. And apparently weeds and clover—as examples not belonging to the grass family—are quietly dismissed from existence as minor nuisances to the idea. Probably it was this use of science, to set the scene and then leave, that won the novel much of its success outside our field.

As fiction, it's an excellent adventure story, in spite of numerous faults. It begins quietly—a virtue that permits the development of tension to be paced properly—and moves forward with power and inevitability. It balances melodrama with underwriting to the advantage of each. It pits man against hostile nature and makes its point (that

---

LESTER DEL REY, who reviews new science-fiction novels for VANGUARD *(and only for VSF) each issue, exploded into the field in 1938; his second story, published the same year, was the classic "Helen O'Loy." He is also the author of one of the finest of all s-f novels, "Nerves" (Ballantine Books), and a number of teen-age novels for Winston. The latest of the Winston books is the handsome "Across the Space Frontier," a factual survey of the coming age of space flight.*

the primary function of life is survival) with a sustained emotional drive on the reader that is all too rare in fiction. While I find none of it very shocking, I have to agree with the *Post* that it's hard to put down and rewarding reading.

Strangely, for a story on this level, its major weakness comes in the handling of character. The women throughout never seem to breathe. Ann, the wife of the leader, has one brief moment of superb realism after a time of horror, but is mostly so flatly insipid that she's incredible; in the end, she is nothing but a vehicle for platitudes that have no place in their world. John, who leads the march, seems more driven than driving; never quite sure of himself, he does the right things without establishing inner conviction. His friend Roger, who could have been a real person, fades quietly into the background until he is only a name.

Yet Christopher does give the story one vital character—and that one is enough. This is Pirrie, the gunsmith, the realist—a man who fits himself to the times and knows what must be done. It is Pirrie who realizes that the mores of the tribe must henceforth apply, and who sees that a tribe must have a leader. It is Pirrie who chooses the leader, and who knows he cannot be the man. Without ever giving us more than the actions of Pirrie, Christopher has produced a marvelously three-dimensional and complex character with the basic simplicity of greatness to make it more complex. This is Pirrie's story, and without him the novel collapses back into platitudinous emotionalism.

In the end, perhaps the weakness of John is best shown by the fact that he can bother thinking about his brother with regret, instead of his thoughts being solely on Pirrie and the destiny Pirrie has carved out for him and his. This end strikes me as a weak sop tossed in to placate the maudlin morality of slick readers. It leaves much to be desired—and without Pirrie, I suppose that is inevitable.

All the faults are fairly obvious—and the virtues of the story are subtle ones of emotional power. But my final verdict is that it's a novel that is head and shoulders above its own weaknesses. If you can afford the hard-cover book, get it; if you can't, don't miss the paperback edition whenever that comes out. Buy!

HIGH VACUUM, by Charles Eric Maine. Ballantine Books, New York. 185pp. 35¢

This paperback original is at the opposite end of the spectrum from Christopher's novel. This is marginal science *fiction*. Science and what passes for extropolation furnish about the only excuse for the novel.

The basic theme here is again that the primary drive in life is for survival, apparently. The first manned moon ship crashes into a crater where life is nearly impossible. One girl and three men try to live in their space suits under lunar conditions, since lethal radiation makes it impossible to stay in the ship. All but one must die before rescue can be accomplished. While not a fresh idea, this is a particularly valid frame for a novel today, when all basic plots dealing with the conquest of space merit careful reëxamination. Unfortunately, this is not a good example of such reëxamination.

The science element dominates the fiction, but only by default. Facts are manhandled, probabilities are ignored, and details are poorly or falsely supplied. It takes the protagonist half the book to discover that sound will travel in a solid as well as in air, though he is a trained engineer and the knowledge is important. (Earlier, Maine writes a scene where sound does *not* apparently travel through a solid.) For some strange reason, the ship takes off *from Earth* to refuel in an orbit; the wastefulness of this in added structural strength and streamlining hardly needs pointing out to anyone who cares to read anything of the works by Wernher von Braun and Willy Ley. The ship lands on a field of uranium so rich that its gamma radiation exceeds permissable dosage within a few hours through the walls of the ship; this is ridiculous—such an incredibly, fantastically rich deposit at the surface of so light a world as Luna is totally unacceptable—and unnecessary, since more ingenious means for making the ship uninhabitable could have been found. Earth sends out supply rockets set to home on the metal of the ship—and never even thinks of having them home on the currently-working radio or radar signals of the ship, which would have made their close arrival a certainty; and, of course, would have ruined the plot "complications"! The men trudge back and forth through the uranium field to the ship for physical needs, but apparently never think of using their metal plate and sealing compounds to line a dugout, tiny comfort station below the surface. And the girl uses up all the air in the ship to burn pages of a log while they're worrying about having oxygen enough to survive—and never thinks that the log could be simply thrown into some crevasse.

All of this inadequate thinking on elementary science and technology in their situation makes many of the plotting devices fail completely; and the inventiveness elsewhere is at a very low level. The characters are puppets, moving to keep things going. The commander is an unsuspecting, fumbling incompetent. The engineer, from whose view we see most of the story, is described in some detail, but he only emerges as someone vaguely unpleasant; he's ruthlessly dedicated to his own survival, but at the crucial moment he can't kill the girl because she's female—even though she's a proven murderer! The surgeon lets himself get a fatal case of gangrene, though the ship is obviously supplied with antibiotics; he never amounts to anything, anyhow, so it doesn't really matter. And the girl, who comes closest to being a person, is a thoroughly unlikeable bitch *who has stowed away*! That device must have taken nerve on the author's part; I've used the old chestnut in a teen-age book, after careful preparation, but I admit I wouldn't have the courage to use it in modern adult science fiction. However, if any of the men had exercised even elementary common sense, her machinations wouldn't have mattered; and the fact that she's duly punished in the end after an obfuscating dream sequence comes as neither a surprise nor a relief. The story is meant to be grim and hard-hitting, but succeeds in being only grimly determined.

The writing, on the whole, is stylistically considerably better than Maine's earlier work. In the passages where it has a chance to say something, it is quite adequate.

Far below Ballantine's usual level of science fiction.

BIG PLANET, by Jack Vance. Avalon Books, New York. 223pp. $2.75.

Like most books from Avalon, this shows evidence of considerable heavy-handed cutting and editing that hasn't improved the 1952 *Startling Stories* novel. Apparently these books are meant for lending libraries where length matters less than number of pages, and the average of less than 200 words to a page doesn't make for any bargain.

Nevertheless, if you haven't read the original, this is worth looking into. Vance bases his tale on a planet larger than Jupiter but of such light elements that the surface gravity is like that of Earth; a world so huge that no central government or full Earth control is possible, where every cult and cockeyed group can find room to experiment. The Earthman Glystra is sent out to investigate one government whose dictator is threatening all of Big Planet. Through duplicity, he is set down 40,000 miles from his headquarters, surrounded by enemies, crackpot cultures, and nobody-knows-what, with only his wits to carry him through.

It makes for an interesting journey, and that's what it is. The characters in the story are adequate, but the real center of interest is the journey across the fascinating lands of Big Planet, where adventures occur regularly, and are given life and sparkle by the quick side-glances at what lies around them. Vance, at his best, has a richness of inventiveness and a rare economy in gaining his effects, and both show well here. I particularly liked the culture of Myrtlesee Fountain with its living oracle doomed to death as the price of true prophecy (all of which is given a logical basis). Properly, this is more of a tale of wonder than a novel, but it's a good one.

If you can't get the original magazine, look around the lending libraries for this book. (Avalon buys rights for a flat price, so you won't be robbing Vance of any royalties.) If you're flush and can find it, you might buy the book; the price is steep for the amount of wordage, but a good tale of this sort is rare.

THE FROZEN YEAR, by James Blish. Ballantine Books, New York. 155pp. 35¢.

This, to my knowledge, is the first book of fiction on the International Geophysical Year, and may well prove to be the best one. And don't let anyone fool you—it *is* science fiction,* even if it's also a bitterly amusing story of the effect of public relations counselling on polar expeditions.

Cole, the narrator, gets mixed up with a publicity-rooting group supposed to be doing observations for the IGY; the director is actually interested in proving a cockeyed theory of meteorite origin, his wife in getting on the front page when not grabbing for relief from frustration. There's a drunken astronomer of sorts, and numerous others to louse things up. By mismanagement, the group winds up in a hell of a fix, is thoroughly discredited for being accidentally right, finds evidence that the meteorite theory was correct, and—as I insist on believing—bumps into a guilt-crazed Martian. While all this goes on, we get some scalpel work on public relations, modern exploration, and just about everything else. We also get an odd warmth and compassion (through vivid, interesting characterization) that I've seldom found before in Blish's work. The science is sound; recent evidence indicates that even the theory of a planet between Mars and Jupiter that blew up may well be a correct one.

To me, the only major weakness comes at the end; this doesn't tie in well with the narrator's jinx fixation, supposedly still operating when the man begins telling the account. And I feel it's a mistake to jump from the closeness of one year ahead, on which the book is based, to a final chapter enough years later for space stations to be in operation. This destroys some of the reality, and isn't really necessary. Sometimes the old rules of unity of time and place make sense, and here the violation of the first leaves a note of unfortunate anticlimax.

Still, as an original novel for 35¢, and one of Blish's and Ballantine's best, it's a quadruple bargain. Buy.

*The author continues to insist that it isn't.—Ed.

THE 13TH IMMORTAL, by Robert Silverberg. 129pp.; THIS FORTRESS WORLD, by James E. Gunn. 189pp. Ace Books, New York. 35¢.

Silverberg's story is an original, having seen no previous publication. The basic idea, however, is one with a considerable tradition behind it—and a tradition that should never have been established, unfortunately.

Essentially, it's a story of a man who must find his destiny without knowing just what it is. He sets out blindly, pushed from pillar to post, stumbling from episode to episode, failing at everything he tries for lack of something better. His only success is in running away—and this he does only with fortuitous help whenever the jam is too tough for him. In the end, it turns out he's the son of the ruler of civilization, destined to take over the rule—and somehow, we're supposed to believe that his experience at failure makes him worthy of the job. The basic idea here is so grotesquely wrong that nothing good can possibly come of it, though many writers have tried to beat the odds.

In this case, Silverberg contributes several nice bits of background. His cybernetic city and logically-established haven for mutants are enjoyable. His characters, limited by the framework, suffer badly, however. The hero is good only as a farmer in the first chapter. Dictator Don Miguel comes to brief life and then fades out of the action. And the mutant, Dawnspear, is excellent—until we find he's only a blind human; we never do learn how he, as a non-mutant, can see without eyes.

I can't help feeling Silverberg would have been well-advised to let this one appear under a pseudonym. He's done much better.

Gunn's novel was introduced by Gnome Press in 1955. It's another of the swashbucklers about an acolyte who finds his monastic order only a false front for a world of intrigue. For those who want escape to a world of fantasy, adventure, mystery and romance, it's a good buy in this form. It's hokum—but pleasant hokum.

Department of Pantropy:
A SOUND OF DIFFERENT DRUMMERS, by Robert Alan Aurthur. Playhouse 90, CBS.

In this original play (starring Sterling Hayden, Diana Lynn and John Ireland), television has finally produced a major science fiction story worth the attention of an adult audience. Aurthur's story is the definitive job on a book-burning future, superior in artistry, honesty and content to anything previously done on this subject. If it's replayed on kinescope or made into a movie, see it. If not, I hope some publisher will have it turned into a book. Congratulations to all concerned!

FAREWELL PARTY

by
Richard Wilson

THE BLUE FELLOW didn't look particularly out of place at the cocktail party. He was properly dressed—tweed jacket, white shirt, tie, all that—but he *was* blue, of course. There were tan people, pasty-white ones, three Negroes, an Indian (Asian) and a Japanese.

It was a farewell party for Massiet of *France-Soir*. A hundred people were crowded into the two-room apartment between Park and Lexington in the Eighties. Lindley had been to fifty like it. There was Suzi, the *chanteuse,* who would be dashing back to the Shubert any minute in her waiting Cadillac for her final number. There was the artists' model with the black sheath gown which inadequately covered her breasts. Lindley tried to think of her name. There was the Japanese who smiled and half-bowed whenever anyone looked at him, still atoning for World War II. And there was the blue fellow.

Lindley forced his way with smiles and how-are-yous and pardon-mes from the hall to the bar. The white-jacketed man from the catering service put three cubes in a glass and poured Scotch till Lindley said "Whoa," then added a courtesy of soda.

Lindley said "Thanks" and started to move away. The blue fellow was blocking his way.

"Sorry," Lindley said. "Oh, hello. Everything all right?"

The blue fellow was holding a glass whose ice had long since melted. He smiled as if to shrug and Lindley said, "Let me get you a fresh one."

He let Lindley hand his glass to the barman. He said nothing. He continued to smile, not as if he were enjoying himself, and not apologetically like the Japanese. It was a masking smile, Lindley thought, a desperate-almost smile.

On impulse he said to the bartender, "Make it a strong one—easy on the soda," and handed it to the blue fellow.

"Are you a friend of Massiet?" Lindley asked him.

The other nodded vigorously. He lifted his glass in salute but didn't drink.

The artists' model was working her way to the bar. She squeezed past Lindley, saying, "Hello, stranger. Divorce yourself from that one, why don't you?"

Lindley was willing, but he'd better remember her name first. "See you later," he said to the girl. "Don't go 'way."

The blue fellow watched the girl go by. He said nothing but his eyes followed her with a sort of yearning appreciation.

"Definitely," Lindley said. He carried on, trying not to seem as if he were cross-examining the fellow. "Stacked, as we say. How do you say it?"

It seemed to him that the blue fellow understood English but couldn't speak it. But he must have a name. He could say that much.

"Look," Lindley said, "we haven't met. My name's Lindley. Jason Lindley. *Cleveland Plain Dealer*. What's yours?"

The other swirled his drink so that the ice tinkled. That was the only sound out of him.

The model—Lindley remembered now that her name was Naomi—made her way back from the bar. She eased past a man from Reuters who tried unsuccessfully to draw her into conversation and stopped next to Lindley. "Got a cigarette?" she asked him.

Lindley supplied a Lucky and Naomi bent enticingly over the match. "Ditch the blue boy," she said. She made a red circle of her mouth and blew smoke in his face. "Let's find a quiet corner and discuss the state of the world."

"Who is he?" Lindley asked her. "Do you know?"

She shrugged, apparently more for the purpose of wiggling the body than providing information. She was extremely physical. "I've found a place to sit down, believe it or not. Don't be too long." Naomi went back through the crowd.

Lindley regretfully transferred his gaze from her disappearing hips to the blue fellow's face.

"Are you in one of the shows?" he asked. The blue might be stage makeup. For instance the French singer, Suzi, was wearing the garish reds and greens which would soften when she was back under the Shubert's spotlights.

But the blue fellow's color didn't seem to be makeup and he made no answer to Lindley's question. His hair was also blue, and Lindley observed for the first time that his ears were pointed at the tops.

Massiet, the guest of honor, made his way through the crush, holding two empty glasses. You met everybody if you stood near the bar, Lindley thought.

"Oh, hello," Massiet said to Lindley. "How are you? Still Plain Dealing?"

"Not at the moment," Lindley said. "Introduce me to your friend."

"My friend?" Massiet looked at the blue fellow. "Oh, hello, *mon ami*. They taking care of you?"

The blue fellow raised the glass

Lindley had refilled for him. He smiled and took a swallow. Lindley noticed now that his teeth were odd, too. They weren't individual, with spaces between them, but seemed to be one complete fixture like an animal's hoof—or like the teeth in a drawing of a smiling girl, all of a piece.

Massiet had worked past them and was behind Lindley now, at the bar. Lindley said to him over his shoulder, "What's his name? Where's he from? Can't he say anything?"

"Who?" Massiet said. "Not so much ice. That's better. Oh, the blue one. I don't know. He drifted in. You know how people do." Massiet worked himself back past them. "Naomi was asking for you, Lindley." He winked. "Wish she'd ask for me."

"Look," Lindley said to the blue fellow. "I've got to go. I hate to be rude, but— Would you mind answering one question?"

The other smiled with his solid teeth and shook his head. Lindley noticed his ears again. The hair that was growing out of them somehow reminded him of tiny wires, like an antenna.

"It'll sound ridiculous, I suppose," Lindley said, "but – are you an Earthman?"

The blue fellow continued to smile but his eyes were no longer focused on Lindley. It was as if he were seeing something that wasn't there. He looked down at his watch. Lindley had just enough of a glimpse of it to see that it didn't have a conventional 12-hour face. Was it 24? Or something else entirely? He couldn't tell.

The blue fellow turned away from Lindley and set his glass down. He found a chair and stood on it. He raised a hand and held it out, palm down, at chest level.

People said "Sh, sh" and turned to face him. The dozens of different conversations died away till the room was almost silent.

The blue fellow stood there,

RICHARD WILSON published his first science-fiction story in 1940. His output since then has been relatively small (at least, as compared with such torrents of prose as his exact contemporary, C. M. Kornbluth). Despite the existence of a Wilson novel, "The Girls From Planet 5" (Ballantine Books), Wilson is primarily a minaturist; he delights in putting a blindingly high polish on an almost invisible fictional point, like a lapidary fanatically cutting facets in a grain of diamond dust. When it is successful, as it often is with Wilson, the method requires the reader to register every word, like poetry — and with similar rewards.

looking across the room. But not at anyone, Lindley noticed. His gaze was on the far wall. He was smiling with a sort of urgency and holding out his hand. He turned the hand palm upward.

There was a tug at Lindley's elbow. It was Naomi.

"Hey," she said. "How about getting out of here?"

"Sh! He's going to say something. Finally."

"No he isn't," Naomi said. "Come on. I'm getting a headache from the smoke."

"Sure he is," Lindley said. "Wait just a minute."

The blue fellow was still standing on the chair, still smiling almost desperately, still gazing at the opposite wall. He gestured with his hand but spoke not a word.

Gradually the hubbub of conversation resumed as the guests turned away from him.

"You mean he isn't going to say anything?" Lindley asked.

"I told you. He never does."

"You sound as if you've seen him do this before."

"Sure I have. He goes to all the parties."

"*I*'ve never seen him," Lindley said.

"You and I don't always go to the same parties, more's the pity," she said. "He's a nut, that's all."

"I don't think he is. I think he actually is communicating in some way but that no one is able to, to—well, to *receive* him. I think he's an alien."

"Sure," Naomi said. "These parties are crawling with aliens. Cosmopolitan as hell."

"I don't mean a foreigner. I mean somebody not from Earth. How about that for a story?"

"Cut it out, Lind. You've been seeing too many horror movies." She began to fidget attractively. "Are you going to come on, or do I have to go home alone?"

"Well, if you put it that way—" He took a last look at the blue fellow. He was still standing on the chair in silence. By now no one was paying the slightest attention to him. "Maybe you're right," Lindley said. "After all, it is my day off."

He went out with Naomi. There probably wasn't any story, and if there was his paper could get it from the wire services. As Naomi put her arm through his and squeezed his hand in the elevator he thought with one last twinge of duty that there might possibly be a very big story. He shrugged and returned Naomi's squeeze.

Now, if it had been a blue girl...

A whole culture afloat, with a savage code to drive it — but not half so savage as what the outcasts found on land.

REAP THE DARK TIDE

by

C. M. Kornbluth

–I–

IT WAS THE SPRING SWARMING OF the plankton; every man and woman and most of the children aboard Grenville's Convoy had a job to do. As the seventy-five gigantic sailing ships ploughed their two degrees of the South Atlantic the fluid that foamed beneath their cutwaters seethed also with life. In the few weeks of the swarming, in the few meters of surface water where sunlight penetrated in sufficient strength to trigger photosynthesis, microscopic spores burst into microscopic plants, were devoured by minute animals which in turn were swept into the maws of barely visible sea monsters almost a tenth of an inch from head to tail; these in turn were fiercely pursued and gobbled in shoals by the fierce little brit, the tiny herring and shrimp that could turn a hundred miles of green water to molten silver before your eyes.

Through the silver ocean of the swarming the Convoy scudded and tacked in great controlled zigs and zags, reaping the silver of the sea in the endlessly reeling bronze nets each ship payed out behind.

The Commodore in *Grenville* did not sleep during the swarming; he and his staff dispatched cutters to scout the swarms, hung on the meterologists' words, digested the endless reports from the scout vessels and toiled through the night to prepare the dawn signal. The mainmast flags might tell the captains "Convoy course five degrees right", or "Two degrees left", or only "Convoy course: no change". On those dawn signals depended the life for the next six months of the million and a quarter souls of the Convoy. It had not happened often, but it had happened that a succession of blunders reduced a Convoy's harvest below the minimum necessary to sustain life. Derelicts were sometimes sighted and salvaged from such convoys; strong-stomached men and women were needed for the first boarding and clearing away of human debris. Cannibalism occurred, an obscene thing one had nightmares about.

The seventy-five captains had their own particular purgatory to endure throughout the harvest, the Sail-Seine Equation. It was their job to balance the push on the sails and the drag of the ballooning seines so that push exceeded drag by just the number of pounds that would keep the ship on course and in station, given every conceivable variation of wind force and direction, temperature of water, consistency of brit, and smoothness of hull. Once the catch was salted down it was customary for the captains to converge on *Grenville* for a roaring feast by way of letdown.

Rank had its privileges. There was no such relief for the captains' Net Officers or their underlings for Operations and Maintenance, or for their Food Officers under whom served the Processing and Stowage people. They merely worked, streaming the nets twenty-four hours a day, keeping them bellied out with lines from mast and outriding gigs, keeping them spooling over the great drum amidships, tending the blades that had to scrape the brit from the nets without damaging the nets, repairing the damage when it did occur, and without interruption of the harvest, flash-cooking the part of the harvest to be cooked, drying the part to be dried, pressing oil from the harvest as required, and stowing what was cooked and dried and pressed where it would not spoil, where it would not alter the trim of the ship, where it would not be pilfered by children. This went on for weeks after the silver had gone thin and patchy against the green, and after the silver had altogether vanished.

The routines of many were not changed at all by the swarming season. The blacksmiths, the sailmakers, the carpenters, the watertenders, to a degree the storekeepers, functioned as before, tending to the fabric of the ship, renewing, replacing, reworking. The ships were things of brass, bronze and unrusting steel. Phosphor bronze strands were woven into net, lines and cables; cordage, masts

---

C. M. KORNBLUTH is a one-man literature. Within a year after his appearance in science fiction in 1940, he was operating under seven pen-names, and in 10 years turned out 43 stories — sometimes by himself, sometimes in collaboration with other writers. In the succeeding seven years he has written 19 books; of these, the most widely known is "The Space Merchants", with Frederik Pohl (Ballantine Books). He is now at work on a 20th, a Civil War novel.

and hull were metal; all were inspected daily by the First Officer and his men and women for the smallest pin-head of corrosion. The smallest pin-head of corrosion could spread; it could send a ship to the bottom before it had done spreading, as the chaplains were fond of reminding worshippers when the ships rigged for church on Sundays. To keep the hellish red of iron rust and the sinister blue of copper rust from invading, the squads of oilers were always on the move, with oil distilled from the catch. The sails and the clothes alone could not be preserved; they wore out. It was for this that the felting machines down below chopped wornout sails and clothing into new fibers and twisted and rolled them with kelp and with glue from the catch into new felt for new sails and clothing.

While the plankton continued to swarm twice a year, Grenville's convoy could continue to sail the South Atlantic, from ten-mile limit to ten-mile limit. Not one of the seventy-five ships in the convoy had an anchor.

The Captain's Party that followed the end of Swarming 283 was slow getting under way. McBee, whose ship was Port Squadron 19, said to Salter of Starboard Squadron 30: "To be frank, I'm too damned exhausted to care whether I ever go to another party, but I didn't want to disappoint the Old Man."

The Commodore, trim and bronzed, not showing his eighty years, was across the great cabin from them greeting new arrivals.

Salter said: "You'll feel differently after a good sleep. It was a great harvest, wasn't it? Enough weather to make it tricky and interesting. Remember 276? *That* was the one that wore me out. A grind, going by the book. But this time, on the fifteenth day my foretopsail was going to go about noon, big rip in her, but I needed her for my S-S balance. What to do? I broke out a balloon spinnaker—now wait a minute, let me tell it first before you throw the book at me—and pumped my fore trim tank out. Presto! No trouble; foretopsail replaced in fifteen minutes."

McBee was horrified. "You could have lost your net!"

"My weatherman absolutely ruled out any sudden squalls."

"Weatherman. You could have lost your net!"

Salter studied him. "Saying that once was thoughtless, McBee. Saying it twice is insulting. Do you think I'd gamble with twenty thousand lives?"

McBee passed his hands over his tired face. "I'm sorry," he said. "I told you I was exhausted. Of course under special circumstances it can be a safe maneuver." He walked to a porthole for a glance at his own ship, the nineteenth in the long echelon behind *Grenville*. Salter stared after him. "Losing one's net" was a phrase that occurred in several proverbs; it stood for abysmal folly. In actuality a ship that lost its phosphor-bronze wire mesh was doomed, and quickly. One could improvise with sails or try to jury-rig a net out of the remaining rigging, but not well enough to feed twenty thousand hands, and no fewer than that were needed for maintenance. Grenville's Convoy had met a derelict which lost its net back before 240; children still told horror stories about it, how the remnants of port and starboard watches, mad to a man, were at war, a war of vicious night forays with knives and clubs.

Salter went to the bar and accepted from the Commodore's steward his first drink of the evening, a steel tumbler of colorless fluid distilled from a fermented mash of sargassum weed. It was about forty per cent alcohol and tasted pleasantly of iodides.

He looked up from his sip and his eyes widened. There was a man in captain's uniform talking with the Commodore and he did not recognize his face. But there had been no promotions lately!

The Commodore saw him looking and beckoned him over. He saluted and then accepted the old man's hand-clasp. "Captain Salter," the Commodore said, "my youngest and rashest, and my best harvester. Salter, this is Captain Degerand of the White Fleet."

Salter frankly gawked. He knew perfectly well that Grenville's Convoy was far from sailing alone upon the seas. On watch he had beheld distant sails from time to time. He was aware that cruising the two-degree belt north of theirs was another convoy and that in the belt south of theirs was still another, in fact that the seaborne population of the world was a constant one billion, eighty million. But never had he expected to meet face to face any of them except the one and a quarter million who sailed under Grenville's flag.

Degerand was younger than he, all deeply tanned skin and flashing pointed teeth. His uniform was perfectly ordinary and very queer. He understood Salter's puzzled look. "It's woven cloth," he said. "The White Fleet was launched several decades after Grenville's. By then they had machinery to reconstitute fibers suitable for spinning and they equipped us with it. It's six of one and half a dozen of the other. I think our sails may last longer than yours, but the looms require a lot of skilled labor when they break down."

The Commodore had left them.

"Are we very different from you?" Salter asked.

Degerand said: "Our differences are nothing. Against the dirt men we are brothers—blood brothers."

The term "dirt men" was discomforting; the juxtaposition with "blood" more so. Apparently he was referring to whoever it was that lived on the continents and islands—a shocking breach of manners, of honor, of faith. The words of The Charter circled through Salter's head. ". . . return for the sea and its bounty . . . renounce and abjure the land from which we . . ." Salter had been ten years old before he knew that there *were* continents and islands. His dismay must have shown on his face.

"They have doomed us," the foreign captain said. "We cannot refit. They have sent us out, each upon our two degrees of ocean in larger or smaller convoys as the richness of the brit dictated, and they have cut us off. To each of us will come the catastrophic storm, the bad harvest, the lost net, and death."

It was Salter's impression that Degerand had said the same words many times before, usually to large audiences.

The Commodore's talker boomed out: "Now hear this!" His huge voice filled the stateroom easily; his usual job was to roar through a megaphone across a league of ocean, supplementing flag and lamp signals. "Now hear this!" he boomed. "There's tuna on the table —big fish for big sailors!"

A grinning steward whisked a felt from the sideboard, and there by Heaven it lay! A great baked fish as long as your leg, smoking hot and trimmed with kelp! A hungry roar greeted it; the captains made for the stack of trays and began to file past the steward, busy with knife and steel.

Salter marvelled to Degerand: "I didn't dream there were any left that size. When you think of the tons of brit that old-timer must have gobbled!"

The foreigner said darkly: "We slew the whales, the sharks, the perch, the cod, the herring—everything that used the sea but us. They fed on brit and one another and concentrated it in firm savory flesh like that, but we were jealous of the energy squandered in the long food chain; we decreed that the chain would stop with the link brit-to-man."

Salter by then had filled a tray. "Brit's more reliable," he said. "A convoy can't take chances on fisherman's luck." He happily bolted a steaming mouthful.

"Safety is not everything," Degerand said. He ate, more slowly than Salter. "Your Commodore said you were a rash seaman."

"He was joking. If he believed that, he would have to remove me from command."

The Commodore walked up to them, patting his mouth with a handkerchief and beaming. "Surprised, eh?" he demanded. "Glasgow's lookout spotted that big fellow yesterday half a kilometer away. He signalled me and I told him to lower and row for him. The boat crew sneaked up while he was browsing and gaffed him clean. Very virtuous of us. By killing him we economize on brit and provide a fitting celebration for my captains. Eat hearty! It may be the last we'll ever see."

Degerand rudely contradicted his senior officer. "They can't be wiped out clean, commodore, not exterminated. The sea is deep. Its genetic potential cannot be destroyed. We merely make temporary alterations of the feeding balance."

"Seen any sperm whale lately?" the Commodore asked, raising his white eyebrows. "Go get yourself another helping, captain, before it's gone." It was a dismissal; the foreigner bowed and went to the buffet.

The Commodore asked: "What do you think of him?"

"He has some extreme ideas," Salter said.

"The White Fleet appears to have gone bad," the old man said. "That fellow showed up on a cutter last week in the middle of harvest wanting my immediate, personal attention. He's on the staff of the White Fleet Commodore. I gather they're all like him. They've got slack; maybe rust has got ahead of them, maybe they're overbreeding. A ship lost its net and they didn't let it go. They cannibalized rigging from the whole fleet to make a net for it."

"But–"

"But–but–but. Of course it was the wrong thing and now they're all suffering. Now they haven't the stomach to draw lots and cut their losses." He lowered his voice. "Their idea is some sort of raid on the Western Continent, that America thing, for steel and bronze and whatever else they find not welded to the deck. It's nonsense, of course, spawned by a few silly-clever people on the staff. The crews will never go along with it. Degerand was sent to invite us in!"

Salter said nothing for a while and then: "I certainly hope we'll have nothing to do with it."

"I'm sending him back at dawn with my compliments, and a negative, and my sincere advice to his Commodore that he drop the whole thing before his own crew hears of it and has him bowspritted." The Commodore gave him a wintry smile. "Such a reply is easy to make, of course, just after concluding an excellent harvest. It might be more difficult to signal a negative if we had a couple of ships unnetted and only enough catch in salt to feed sixty per cent of the hands. Do you think you could give the hard answer under those circumstances?"

"I think so, sir."

The Commodore walked away, his face enigmatic. Salter thought he knew what was going on. He had been given one small foretaste of top command. Perhaps he was being groomed for Commodore—not to succeed the old man, surely, but his successor.

McBee approached, full of big

fish and drink. "Foolish thing I said," he stammered. "Let's have drink, forget about it, eh?"

He was glad to.

"Damn fine seaman!" McBee yelled after a couple more drinks. "Best little captain in the Convoy! Not a scared old crock like poor old McBee, 'fraid of every puff of wind!"

And then he had to cheer up McBee until the party began to thin out. McBee fell asleep at last and Salter saw him to his gig before boarding his own for the long row to the bobbing masthead lights of his ship.

Starboard Squadron Thirty was at rest in the night. Only the slowly-moving oil lamps of the women on their ceaseless rust patrol were alive. The brit catch, dried, came to some seven thousand tons. It was a comfortable margin over the 5,670 tons needed for six months' full rations before the autumnal swarming and harvest. The trim tanks along the keel had been pumped almost dry by the ship's current prison population as the cooked and dried and salted cubes were stored in the glass-lined warehouse tier; the gigantic vessel rode easily on a swelling sea before a Force One westerly breeze.

Salter was exhausted. He thought briefly of having his cox'n whistle for a bosun's chair so that he might be hauled at his ease up the fifty-yard cliff that was the hull before them, and dismissed the idea with regret. Rank hath its privileges and also its obligations. He stood up in the gig, jumped for the ladder and began the long climb. As he passed the portholes of the cabin tiers he virtuously kept eyes front, on the bronze plates of the hull inches from his nose. Many couples in the privacy of their double cabins would be celebrating the end of the back-breaking, night-and-day toil. One valued privacy aboard the ship; one's own 648 cubic feet of cabin, one's own porthole, acquired an almost religious meaning, particularly after the weeks of swarming cooperative labor.

Taking care not to pant, he finished the climb with a flourish, springing onto the flush deck. There was no audience. Feeling a little ridiculous and forsaken, he walked aft in the dark with only the wind and the creak of the rigging in his ears. The five great basket masts strained silently behind their breeze-filled sails; he paused a moment beside Wednesday mast, huge as a redwood, and put his hands on it to feel the power that vibrated in its steel latticework.

Six intent women went past, their hand lamps sweeping the deck; he jumped, though they never noticed him. They were in something like a trance state while on their tour of duty. Normal courtesies were suspended for them; with their work began the job of survival. One thousand women, five per cent of the ship's company, inspected night and day for corrosion. Sea water is a vicious solvent and the ship had to live in it; fanaticism was the answer.

His stateroom above the rudder waited; the hatchway to it glowed a hundred feet down the deck with the light of a wasteful lantern. After harvest, when the tanks brimmed with oil, one type acted as though the tanks would brim forever. The captain wearily walked around and over a dozen stay-ropes to the hatchway and blew out the lamp. Before descending he took a mechanical look around the deck; all was well–

Except for a patch of paleness at the fantail.

"Will this day never end?" he asked the darkened lantern and went to the fantail. The patch was a little girl in a night dress wandering aimlessly over the deck, her thumb in her mouth. She seemed to be about two years old, and was more than half asleep. She could have gone over the railing in a moment; a small wail, a small splash–

He picked her up like a feather. "Who's your daddy, princess?" he asked.

"Dunno," she grinned. The devil she didn't! It was too dark to read her ID necklace and he was too tired to light the lantern. He trudged down the deck to the crew of inspectors. He said to their chief: "One of you get this child back to her parents' cabin," and held her out.

The chief was indignant. "Sir, we are on watch!"

"File a grievance with the Commodore if you wish. Take the child."

One of the rounder women did, and made cooing noises while her chief glared. "Bye-bye, princess," the captain said. "You ought to be keel-hauled for this, but I'll give you another chance."

"Bye-bye," the little girl said, waving, and the captain went yawning down the hatchway to bed.

His stateroom was luxurious by the austere standards of the ship. It was equal to six of the standard nine-by-nine cabins in volume, or to three of the double cabins for couples. These however had something he did not. Officers above the rank of lieutenant were celibate. Experience had shown that this was the only answer to nepotism, and nepotism was a luxury which no convoy could afford. It meant, sooner or later, inefficient command. Inefficient command meant, sooner or later, death.

Because he thought he would not sleep, he did not.

Marriage. Parenthood. What a strange business it must be! To share a bed with a wife, a cabin with two children decently behind their screen for sixteen years . . . what did one talk about in bed? His last mistress had hardly talked at all, except with her eyes. When these showed signs that she was falling in love with him, Heaven knew why, he broke with her as quietly as possible and since then irritably rejected the thought of acquiring a successor. That had been two years ago when he was 38, and already beginning to feel like a cabin-crawler fit only to be dropped over the fantail into the wake. An old lecher, a roué, a *user* of women. Of course she had talked a little; what did they have in common to talk about? With a wife ripening beside him, with children to share, it would have been different. That pale, tall quiet girl deserved better than he could give; he hoped she was decently married now in a double cabin, perhaps already heavy with the first of her two children.

A whistle squeaked above his head; somebody was blowing into one of the dozen speaking tubes clustered against the bulkhead. Then a push-wire popped open the steel lid of Tube Seven, Signals. He resignedly picked up the flexible reply tube and said into it: "This is the captain. Go ahead."

"*Grenville* signals Force Three squall approaching from astern, sir."

"Force Three squall from astern. Turn out the fore-starboard watch. Have them reef sail to Condition Charlie."

"Fore-starboard watch, reef sail to Condition Charlie, aye-aye."

"Execute."

"Aye-aye, sir." The lid of Tube Seven, Signals, popped shut. At once he heard the distant, penetrating shrill of the pipe, the faint vibration as one sixth of the deck crew began to stir in their cabins, awaken, hit the deck bleary-eyed, begin to trample through the corridors and up the hatchways to the deck. He got up himself and pulled on clothes, yawning. Reefing from Condition Fox to Condition Charlie was no serious matter, not even in the dark, and Walters on watch was a good officer. But he'd better have a look.

Being flush-decked, the ship offered him no bridge. He conned her from the "first top" of Friday mast, the rearmost of her five. The "first top" was a glorified crow's nest fifty feet up the steel basketwork of that great tower; it afforded him a view of all masts and spars in one glance.

He climbed to his command post too far gone for fatigue. A full moon now lit the scene; good. That much less chance of a green topman stepping on a ratline that would prove to be a shadow and hurtling two hundred feet to the deck. That much more snap in the reefing; that much sooner it would be over. Suddenly he was sure he would be able to sleep if he ever got back to bed again.

He turned for a look at the bronze, moonlit heaps of the great net on the fantail. Within a week it would be cleaned and oiled; within two weeks stowed below in the cable tier, safe from wind and weather.

The regiments of the fore-starboard watch swarmed up the masts from Monday to Friday, swarmed out along the spars as bosun's whistles squealed out the drill—

The squall struck.

Wind screamed and tore at him; the captain flung his arms around a stanchion. Rain pounded down upon his head and the ship reeled in a vast, slow curtsey, port to starboard. Behind him there was a metal sound as the bronze net shifted inches sideways, back.

The sudden clouds had blotted out the moon; he could not see the men who swarmed along the yards but with sudden terrible clarity he felt through the soles of his feet what they were doing. They were clawing their way through the sail-reefing drill, blinded and deafened by sleety rain and wind. They were out of phase by now; they were no longer trying to shorten sail equally on each mast; they were trying to get the thing done and descend. The wind screamed in his face as he turned and clung. Now they were ahead of the job on Monday and Tuesday masts, behind the job on Thursday and Friday masts.

So the ship was going to pitch. The wind would catch it unequally and it would kneel in prayer, the cutwater plunging with a great, deep stately obeisance down into the fathoms of ocean, the stern soaring slowly, ponderously, into the air until the topmost rudder-trunnion streamed a hundred-foot cascade into the boiling froth of the wake.

That was half the pitch. It happened, and the captain clung, groaning aloud. He heard above the screaming wind loose gear rattling on the deck, clashing forward in an avalanche. He heard a heavy clink at the stern and bit his lower lip until it ran with blood that the tearing cold rain flooded from his chin.

The pitch reached its maximum and the second half began, after interminable moments when she seemed frozen at a five-degree angle forever. The cutwater rose, rose, rose, the bowsprit blocked out horizon stars, the loose gear countercharged astern in a crushing tide of bales, windlass cranks, water-breakers, stilling coils, steel sun reflectors, lashing tails of bronze rigging—

Into the heaped piles of the net, straining at its retainers on the two great bollards that took root in the keel itself four hundred feet below. The energy of the pitch hurled the belly of the net open, crashing, into the sea. The bollards held for a moment.

A retainer cable screamed and snapped like a man's back, and then the second cable broke. The roaring slither of the bronze links thundering over the fantail shook the ship.

The squall ended as it had come; the clouds scudded on and the moon bared itself, to shine on a deck scrubbed clean. The net was lost.

Captain Salter looked down the fifty feet from the rim of the crow's nest and thought: I should jump. It would be quicker that way.

But he did not. He slowly began to climb down the ladder to the bare deck.

— II —

Having no electrical equipment, the ship was necessarily a representative republic rather than a democracy. Twenty thousand people can discuss and decide only with the aid of microphones, loudspeakers and rapid calculators to balance the ayes and noes. With lungpower the only means of communication and an abacus in a clerk's hands the only tallying device, certainly no more than fifty people can talk together and make sense, and there are pessimists who say the number is closer to five than fifty. The Ship's Council that met at dawn on the fantail numbered fifty.

It was a beautiful dawn; it lifted the heart to see salmon sky, iridescent sea, spread white sails of the convoy ranged in a great slanting line across sixty miles of oceanic blue.

It was the kind of dawn for which one lived—a full catch salted down, the water-butts filled, the evaporators trickling from their thousand tubes nine gallons each sunrise to sunset, wind enough for easy steerageway and a pretty spread of sail. These were the rewards. One hundred and forty-one years ago Grenville's Convoy had been launched at Newport News, Virginia, to claim them.

Oh, the high adventure of the launching! The men and women who had gone aboard thought themselves heroes, conquerors of nature, self-sacrificers for the glory of NEMET! But NEMET meant only Northeastern Metropolitan Area, one dense warren that stretched from Boston to Newport, built up and dug down, sprawling westward, gulping Pittsburgh without a pause, beginning to peter out past Cincinnati.

The first generation asea clung and sighed for the culture of NEMET, consoled itself with its patriotic sacrifice; any relief was better than none at all, and Grenville's Convoy had drained one and a quarter million population from the huddle. They were immigrants into the sea; like all immigrants they longed for the Old Country. Then the second generation. Like all second generations they had no patience with the old people or their tales. *This* was real, this sea, this gale, this rope! Then the third generation. Like all third generations it felt a sudden desperate hollowness and lack of identity. What was real? Who are we? What is NEMET which we have lost? But by then grandfather and grandmother could only mumble vaguely; the cultural heritage was gone, squandered in three generations, spent forever. As always, the fourth generation did not care.

And those who sat in counsel on the fantail were members of the fifth and sixth generations. They knew all there was to know about life. Life was the hull and masts, the sail and rigging, the net and the evaporators. Nothing more. *Nothing less.* Without masts there was no life. Nor was there life without the net.

The ship's council did not command; command was reserved to the captain and his officers. The council governed, and on occasion tried criminal cases. During the black Winter Without Harvest eighty years before it had decreed euthanasia for all persons over sixty-three years of age and for one out of twenty of the other adults aboard. It had rendered bloody judgment on the ringleaders of Peale's Mutiny. It had sent them into the wake and Peale himself had been bowspritted, given the maritime equivalent of crucifixion. Since then no megalomaniacs had decided to make life interesting for their shipmates, so Peale's long agony had served its purpose.

The fifty of them represented every department of the ship and every age-group. If there was wisdom abroad, it was concentrated there on the fantail. But there was little to say.

The eldest of them, Retired Sailmaker Hodgins, presided. Venerably bearded, still strong of voice, he told them:

"Shipmates, our accident has come. We are dead men. Decency demands that we do not spin out the struggle and sink into—unlawful eatings. Reason tells us that we cannot survive. What I propose is an honorable voluntary death for us all, and the legacy of our ship's fabric to be divided among the remainder of the convoy at the discretion of the Commodore."

He had little hope of his old man's viewpoint prevailing. The Chief Inspector rose at once. She had only three words to say: "*Not my children.*"

Women's heads nodded grimly, and men's with resignation. Decency and duty and common sense were all very well until you ran up against that steel bulkhead. *Not my children.*

A brilliant young chaplain asked: "Has the question even been raised as to whether a collection among the fleet might not provide cordage enough to improvise a net?"

Captain Salter should have answered that, but he, murderer of the twenty thousand souls in his care, could not speak. He nodded jerkily at his signals officer.

Lieutenant Zwingli temporized by taking out his signals slate and pretending to refresh his memory. He said: "At 0035 today a lamp signal was made to *Grenville* advising that our net was lost. *Grenville* replied as follows: 'Effective now, your ship no longer part of convoy. Have no recommendations. Personal sympathy and regrets. Signed, Commodore.' "

Captain Salter found his voice. "I've sent a couple of other messages to *Grenville* and to our neighboring vessels. They do not reply. This is as it should be. We are no longer part of the convoy. Through our own—lapse—we have become a drag on the convoy. We cannot look to it for help. I have no word of condemnation for anybody. This is how life is."

The chaplain folded his hands and began to pray inaudibly.

And then a council member spoke whom Captain Salter knew in another role. It was Jewel Flyte, the tall, pale girl who had been his mistress two years ago. She must be serving as an alternate, he thought, looking at her with new eyes. He did not know she was even that; he had avoided her since then. And no, she was not married; she wore no ring. And neither was her hair drawn back in the semi-official style of the semi-official voluntary celibates, the super-patriots (or simply sex-shy people, or dislikers of children) who surrendered their right to reproduce for the good of the ship (or their own convenience). She was simply a girl in the uniform of a—a what? He had to think hard before he could match the badge over her breast to a department. She was Ship's Archivist with her crossed key and quill, an obscure clerk and shelf-duster under — far under! — the Chief of Yeomen Writers. She must have been elected alternate by the Yeomen in a spasm of sympathy for her blind-alley career.

"My job," she said in her calm steady voice, "is chiefly to search for precedents in the Log when unusual events must be recorded and nobody recollects offhand the form in which they should be recorded. It is one of those provoking jobs which must be done by someone but which cannot absorb the full time of a person. I have therefore had many free hours of actual working time. I have also remained unmarried and am not inclined to sports or games. I tell you this so you may believe me when I say that during the past two years I have read the Ship's Log in its entirety."

There was a little buzz. Truly an astonishing, and an astonishingly pointless, thing to do! Wind and weather, storms and calms, messages and meetings and censuses, crimes, trials and punishments of a hundred and forty-one years; what a bore!

"Something I read," she went on,

"may have some bearing on our dilemma." She took a slate from her pocket and read: "Extract from the Log dated June 30th, Convoy Year 72. 'The Shakespeare-Joyce-Melville Party returned after dark in the gig. They had not accomplished any part of their mission. Six were dead of wounds; all bodies were recovered. The remaining six were mentally shaken but responded to our last ataractics. They spoke of a new religion ashore and its consequences on population. I am persuaded that we seabornes can no longer relate to the continentals. The clandestine shore trips will cease.' The entry is signed 'Scolley, Captain'."

A man named Scolley smiled for a brief proud moment. His ancestor! And then like the others he waited for the extract to make sense. Like the others he found that it would not do so.

Captain Salter wanted to speak, and wondered how to address her. She had been "Jewel" and they all knew it; could he call her "Yeoman Flyte" without looking like, being, a fool? Well, if he was fool enough to lose his net he was fool enough to be formal with an ex-mistress. "Yeoman Flyte," he said, "where does the extract leave us?"

In her calm voice she told them all: "Penetrating the few obscure words, it appears to mean that until Convoy Year 72 the Charter was regularly violated, with the connivance of successive captains. I suggest that we consider violating it once more, to survive."

The Charter. It was a sort of ground-swell of their ethical life, learned early, paid homage every Sunday when they were rigged for church. It was inscribed in phosphor bronze plates on Monday mast of every ship at sea, and the wording was always the same.

IN RETURN FOR THE SEA AND ITS BOUNTY WE RENOUNCE AND ABJURE FOR OURSELVES AND OUR DESCENDANTS THE LAND FROM WHICH WE SPRUNG: FOR THE COMMON GOOD OF MAN WE SET SAIL FOREVER.

At least half of them were unconsciously murmuring the words.

Retired Sailmaker Hodgins rose, shaking. "Blasphemy!" he said. "The woman should be bowsprittedl!"

The chaplain said thoughtfully: "I know a little more about what constitutes blasphemy than Sailmaker Hodgins, I believe, and assure you that he is mistaken. It is a superstitious error to believe that there is any religious sanction for the Charter. It is no ordinance of God but a contract between men."

"It is a Revelation!" Hodgins shouted. "A Revelation! It is the newest testament! It is God's finger pointing the way to the clean hard life at sea, away from the grubbing and filth, from the overbreeding and the sickness!"

That was a common view.

"What about my children?" demanded the Chief Inspector. "Does God want them to starve or be—be—" She could not finish the question, but the last unspoken word of it rang in all their minds.

Eaten.

Aboard some ships with an accidental preponderance of the elderly, aboard other ships where some blazing personality generations back had raised the Charter to a powerful cult, suicide might have been voted. Aboard other ships where nothing extraordinary had happened in six generations, where things had been easy and the knack and tradition of hard decision-making had been lost, there might have been confusion and inaction and the inevitable degeneration into savagery. Aboard Salter's ship the Council voted to send a small party ashore to investigate. They used every imaginable euphemism to describe the action, took six hours to make up their minds, and sat at last on the fantail cringing a little, as if waiting for a thunderbolt.

The shore party would consist of Salter, Captain; Flyte, Archivist; Pemberton, Junior Chaplain; Graves, Chief Inspector.

Salter climbed to his conning top on Friday mast, consulted a chart from the archives, and gave the order through speaking tube to the tiller gang: "Change course red four degrees."

The repeat came back incredulously.

"Execute," he said. The ship creaked as eighty men heaved the tiller; imperceptibly at first the wake began to curve behind them.

Ship Starboard 30 departed from its ancient station; across a mile of sea the bosun's whistles could be heard from Starboard 31 as she put on sail to close the gap.

"They might have signaled something," Salter thought, dropping his glasses at last on his chest. But the masthead of Starboard 31 remained bare of all but its commission pennant.

He whistled up his signals officer and pointed to their own pennant. "Take that thing down," he said hoarsely, and went below to his cabin.

The new course would find them at last riding off a place the map described as New York City.

—III—

Salter issued what he expected would be his last commands to Lieutenant Zwingli; the whaleboat was waiting in its davits; the other three were in it.

"You'll keep your station here as well as you're able," said the captain. "If we live, we'll be back in a couple of months. Should we not return, that would be a potent argument against beaching the ship and attempting to live off the continent—but it will be your problem then and not mine."

They exchanged salutes. Salter sprang into the whaleboat, signalled the deck hands standing by at the ropes and the long creaking descent began.

Salter, Captain; age 40; unmarried *ex officio*; parents Clayton Salter, master instrument maintenanceman, and Eva Romano, chief dietician; selected from dame school age ten for A Track training; seamanship school certificate at age 16, navigation certificate at age 20, First Lieutenants School age 24, commissioned ensign age 24; lieutenant at 30, commander at 32; commissioned captain and succeeded to command of Ship Starboard 30 the same year.

Flyte, Archivist, age 25; unmarried; parents Joseph Flyte, entertainer, and Jessie Waggoner, entertainer; completed dame school age 14, B Track training, Yeoman's School certificate at age 16, Advanced Yeoman's School certificate at age 18, Efficiency rating, 3.5.

Pemberton, Chaplain, age 30; married to Riva Shields, nurse; no children by choice; parents Will Pemberton, master distiller-watertender, and Agnes Hunt, feltermachinist's mate; completed dame school age 12, B Track training, Divinity School Certificate at age 20; mid-starboard watch curate, later forestarboard chaplain.

Graves, chief inspector, age 34, married to George Omany, blacksmith third class; two children; completed dame school age 15, Inspectors School Certificate at age 16; inspector third class, second class, first class, master inspector, then chief. Efficiency rating, 4.0; three commendations.

Versus the Continent of North America.

They all rowed for an hour; then a shoreward breeze came up and Salter stepped the mast. "Ship your oars," he said, and then wished he dared countermand the order. Now they would have time to think of what they were doing.

The very water they sailed was different in color from the deep water they knew, and different in its way of moving. The life in it—

"Great God!" Mrs. Graves cried, pointing astern.

It was a huge fish, half the size of their boat. It surfaced lazily and slipped beneath the water in an uninterrupted arc. They had seen steel-grey skin, not scales, and a great slit of a mouth.

Salter said, shaken: "Unbelievable. Still, I suppose in the unfished offshore waters a few of the large forms survive. And the intermediate sizes to feed them—" And footlong smaller sizes to feed *them,* and—

Was it mere arrogant presumption that Man had permanently changed the life of the sea?

The afternoon sun slanted down and the tip of Monday mast sank below the horizon's curve astern;

the breeze that filled their sail bowled them towards a mist which wrapped vague concretions they feared to study too closely. A shadowed figure huge as a mast with one arm upraised; behind its blocks and blocks of something solid.

"This is the end of the sea," said the captain.

Mrs. Graves said what she would have said if a silly under-inspector had reported to her blue rust on steel: "Nonsense!" Then, stammering: "I beg your pardon, captain. Of course you are correct."

"But it sounded strange," Chaplain Pemberton said helpfully. "I wonder where they all are?"

Jewel Flyte said in her quiet way: "We should have passed over the discharge from waste tubes before now. They used to pump their waste through tubes under the sea and discharge it several miles out. It colored the water and it stank. During the first voyaging years the captains knew it was time to tack away from land by the color and the bad smell."

"They must have improved their disposal system by now," Salter said, "It's been centuries."

His last word hung in the air.

The chaplain studied the mist from the bow. It was impossible to deny it; the huge thing was an Idol. Rising from the bay of a great city, an Idol, and a female one—the worst kind! "I thought they had them only in High Places," he muttered, discouraged.

Jewel Flyte understood. "I think it has no religious significance," she said. "It's a sort of—huge piece of scrimshaw."

Mrs. Graves studied the vast thing and saw in her mind the glyphic arts as practiced at sea: compacted kelp shaved and whittled into little heirloom boxes, miniature portrait busts of children. She decided that Yeoman Flyte had a dangerously wild imagination. Scrimshaw! Tall as a mast!

There should be some commerce, thought the captain. Boats going to and fro. The Place ahead was plainly an island, plainly inhabited; goods and people should be going to it and coming from it. Gigs and cutters and whaleboats should be plying this bay and those two rivers; at that narrow bit they should be lined up impatiently waiting, tacking and riding under sea anchors and furled sails. There was nothing but a few white birds that shrilled nervously at their solitary boat.

The blocky concretions were emerging from the haze; they were sunset-red cubes with regular black eyes dotting them; they were huge dice laid down side by side by side, each as large as a ship, each therefore capable of holding twenty thousand persons.

Where were they all?

The breeze and the tide drove them swiftly through the neck of water where a hundred boats should be waiting. "Furl the sail," said

Salter. "Out oars."

With no sounds but the whisper of the oarlocks, the cries of the white birds and the slapping of the wavelets they rowed under the shadow of the great red dice to a dock, one of a hundred teeth projecting from the island's rim.

"Easy the starboard oars," said Salter; "handsomely the port oars. Up oars. Chaplain, the boat hook." He had brought them to a steel ladder; Mrs. Graves gasped at the red rust thick on it. Salter tied the painter to a corroded brass ring. "Come along," he said, and began to climb.

When the four of them stood on the iron-plated dock Pemberton, naturally, prayed. Mrs. Graves followed the prayer with half her attention or less; the rest she could not divert from the shocking slovenliness of the prospect—rust, dust, litter, neglect. What went on in the mind of Jewel Flyte her calm face did not betray. And the captain scanned those black windows a hundred yards inboard—no; inland!—and waited and wondered.

They began to walk to them at last, Salter leading. The sensation underfoot was strange and dead, tiring to the arches and the thighs.

The huge red dice were not as insane close-up as they had appeared from a distance. They were thousand-foot cubes of brick, the stuff that lined ovens. They were set back within squares of green, cracked surfacing which Jewel Flyte named "cement" or "concrete" from some queer corner of her erudition.

There was an entrance, and written over it: THE HERBERT BROWNELL JR. MEMORIAL HOUSES. A bronze plaque shot a pang of guilt through them all as they thought of The Compact, but its words were different and ignoble.

NOTICE TO ALL TENANTS

A Project Apartment is a Privilege and not a Right. Daily Inspection is the Cornerstone of the Project. Attendance at Least Once a Week at the Church of Synagogue of your Choice is Required for Families wishing to remain in Good Standing; Proof of Attendance must be presented on Demand. Possession of Tobacco or Alcohol will be considered Prima Facie Evidence of Undesireability. Excessive Water Use, Excessive Energy Use and Food Waste will be Grounds for Desireability Review. The speaking of Languages other than American by persons over the Age of Six will be considered Prima Facie Evidence of Nonassimilability, though this shall not be construed to prohibit Religious Ritual in Languages other than Amercan.

Below it stood another plaque in paler bronze, an afterthought:

None of the foregoing shall

be construed to condone the Practice of Depravity under the Guise of Religion by Whatever Name, and all Tenants are warned that any Failure to report the Practice of Depravity will result in summary Eviction and Denunciation.

Around this later plaque some hand had painted with crude strokes of a tar brush a sort of anatomical frame at which they stared in wondering disgust.

At last Pemberton said: "They were a devout people." Nobody noticed the past tense, it sounded so right.

"Very sensible," said Mrs. Graves. "No nonsense about them."

Captain Salter privately disagreed. A ship run with such dour coercion would founder in a month; could land people be that much different?

Jewel Flyte said nothing, but her eyes were wet. Perhaps she was thinking of scared little human rats dodging and twisting through the inhuman maze of great fears and minute rewards.

"After all," said Mrs. Graves, "It's nothing but a Cabin Tier. We have cabins and so had they. Captain, might we have a look?"

"This *is* a reconnaissance," Salter shrugged. They went into a littered lobby and easily recognized an elevator which had long ago ceased to operate; there were many hand-run dumbwaiters at sea.

A gust of air flapped a sheet of printed paper across the chaplain's ankles; he stooped to pick it up with a kind of instinctive outrage —leaving paper unsecured, perhaps to blow overboard and be lost forever to the ship's economy! Then he flushed at his silliness. "So much to unlearn," he said, and spread the paper to look at it. A moment later he crumpled it in a ball and hurled it from him as hard and as far as he could, and wiped his hands with loathing on his jacket. His face was utterly shocked.

The others stared. It was Mrs. Graves who went for the paper.

"Don't look at it," said the chaplain.

"I think she'd better," Salter said.

The maintenancewoman spread the paper, studied it and said: "Just some nonsense. Captain, what do you make of it?"

It was a large page torn from a book, and on it were simple polychrome drawing and some lines of verse in the style of a child's first reader. Salter repressed a shocked guffaw. The picture was of a little boy and a little girl quaintly dressed locked in murderous combat, using teeth and nails. "*Jack and Jill went up the hill,*" said the text, "*to fetch a pail of water. She threw Jack down and broke his crown; it was a lovely slaughter.*"

Jewel Flyte took the page from his hands. All she said was, after a long pause: "I suppose they couldn't start them too young."

She dropped the page and she too wiped her hands.

"Come along," the captain said. "We'll try the stairs."

The stairs were dust, rat-dung, cobwebs and two human skeletons. Murderous knuckledusters fitted loosely the bones of the two right hands. Salter hardened himself to pick up one of the weapons, but could not bring himself to try it on. Jewel Flyte said apologetically: "Please be careful, captain. It might be poisoned. That seems to be the way they were."

Salter froze. By God, but the girl was right! Delicately, handling the spiked steel thing by its edges, he held it up. Yes; stains—it *would* be stained, and perhaps with poison also. He dropped it into the thoracic cage of one skeleton and said: "Come on." They climbed in quest of a dusty light from above; it was a doorway onto a corridor of many doors. There was evidence of fire and violence. A barricade of queer pudgy chairs and divans had been built to block the corridor, and had been breached. Behind it were sprawled three more heaps of bones.

"They have no heads," the chaplain said hoarsely. "Captain Salter, this is not a place for human beings. We must go back to the ship, even if it means honorable death. This is not a place for human beings."

"Thank you, chaplain," said Salter. "You've cast your vote. Is anybody with you?"

"Kill your own children, chaplain," said Mrs. Graves. "Not mine."

Jewel Flyte gave the chaplain a sympathetic shrug and said: "No."

One door stood open, its lock shattered by blows of a fire axe. Salter said: "We'll try that one." They entered into the home of an ordinary middle-class death-worshipping family as it had been a century ago, in the one hundred and thirty-first year of Merdeka the Chosen.

— IV —

Merdeka the Chosen, the All-Foreigner, the Ur-Alien, had never intended any of it. He began as a retail mail-order vendor of movie and television stills, eight-by-ten glossies for the fan trade. It was a hard dollar; you had to keep an immense stock to cater to a tottery Mae Bush admirer, to the pony-tailed screamer over Rip Torn, and to everybody in between. He would have no truck with pinups. "Dirty, lascivious pictures!" he snarled when broadly-hinting letters arrived. "Filth! Men and women kissing, ogling, pawing each other! Orgies! Bah!" Merdeka kept a neutered dog, a spayed cat, and a crumpled uncomplaining housekeeper who was technically his wife. He was poor; he was very poor. Yet he never neglected his charitable duties, contributing every year to the Planned Parenthood Federation and the Midtown Hysterectomy Clinic.

They knew him in the Third Avenue saloons where he talked every night, arguing with Irishmen, sometimes getting asked outside to be knocked down. He let them knock him down, and sneered from the pavement. Was *this* their argument? *He* could argue. He spewed facts and figures and clichés in unanswerable profusion. Hell, man, the Russians'll have a bomb base on the moon in two years and in two years the Army and the Air Force will still be beating each other over the head with pigs' bladders. Just a minute, let me tell you: the goddammycin's making idiots of us all; do you know of any children born in the past two years that're healthy? And: 'flu be go to hell; it's our own germ warfare from Camp Crowder right outside Baltimore that got out of hand, and it happened the week of the 24th. And: The human animal's obsolete; they've proved at M.I.T., Steinwitz and Kohlmann *proved* that the human animal cannot survive the current radiation levels. And: enjoy your lung-cancer, friend; for every automobile and its stinking exhaust there will be two-point-seven-oh-three cases of lung cancer, and we've got to have our automobiles, don't we? And: delinquency my foot; they're insane and it's got to the point where the economy cannot support mass insanity; they've got to be castrated; it's the only way. And: they should dig up the body of Metchnikoff and throw it to the dogs; he's the degenerate who invented venereal prophylaxis and since then vice without punishment has run hog-wild through the world; what we need on the streets is a few of those old-time locomotor ataxia cases limping and drooling to show the kids where vice leads.

He didn't know where he came from. The delicate New York way of establishing origins is to ask: "Merdeka, hah? What kind of a name is that now?" And to this he would reply that he wasn't a lying Englishman or a loud-mouthed Irishman or a perverted Frenchman or a chiseling Jew or a barbarian Russian or a toadying German or a thickheaded Scandihoovian, and if his listener didn't like it, what did he have to say in reply?

He was from an orphanage, and the legend at the orphanage was that a policeman had found him, two hours old, in a garbage can coincident with the death by hemmorrhage on a trolley car of a luetic young woman whose named appeared to be Merdeka and who had certainly been recently delivered of a child. No other facts were established, but for generation after generation of orphanage inmates there was great solace in having one of their number who indisputably had got off to a worse start than they.

A watershed of his career occurred when he noticed that he was, for the seventh time that year, re-ordering prints of scenes from Mr. Howard Hughes' production *The Outlaw*. These were not the off-the-bust stills of Miss Jane Russell, surprisingly, but were group scenes of Miss Russell suspended by her wrists and about to be whipped. Merdeka studied the scene, growled "Give it to the bitch!" and doubled the order. It sold out. He canvassed his files for other whipping and torture stills from *Desert Song*-type movies, made up a special assortment, and it sold out within a week. Then he knew.

The man and the opportunity had come together, for perhaps the fiftieth time in history. He hired a model and took the first specially posed pictures himself. They showed her cringing from a whip, tied to a chair with a clothesline, and herself brandishing the whip.

Within two months Merdeka had cleared six thousand dollars and he put every cent of it back into more photographs and direct-mail advertising. Within a year he was big enough to attract the post-office obscenity people. He went to Washington and screamed in their faces: "My stuff isn't obscene and I'll sue you if you bother me, you stinking bureaucrats! You show me one breast, you show me one behind, you show me one human being touching another in my pictures! You can't and you know you can't! I don't believe in sex and I don't push sex, so you leave me the hell alone! Life is pain and suffering and being scared so people like to look at my pictures; my pictures are about *them*, the scared little jerks! You're just a bunch of goddam perverts if you think there's anything dirty about my pictures!"

He had them there; Merdeka's girls always wore at least full panties, bras and stockings; he had them there. The Post-office obscenity people were vaguely positive that there was *something* wrong with pictures of beautiful women tied down to be whipped or burned with hot irons, but what?

The next year they tried to get him on his income tax; those deductions for the Planned Parenthood Federation and the Midtown Hysterectomy Clinic were preposterous, but he proved them with canceled checks to the last nickel. "In fact," he indignantly told them, "I spend a lot of time at the Clinic and sometimes they let me watch the operations. *That's* how highly they think of me at the Clinic."

The next year he started *DEATH: the Weekly Picture Magazine* with the aid of a half-dozen bright young grads from new Harvard School of Communicationeering. As *DEATH's* Communicator in Chief (only yesterday he would have been its Publisher, and only fifty years before he would have been its Editor) he slumped biliously in a pigskin-panelled office, peering suspiciously at the closed-circuit TV screen which had a hundred wired eyes throughout *DEATH's* offices, sometimes growling over the voice circuit: "You! What's your name? Boland? You're through, Boland. Pick up your time at the paymaster." For any reason; for no reason. He was a living legend in his narrow-lapel charcoal flannel suit and stringy bullfighter neckties; the bright young men in their Victorian Revival frock coats and pearl-pinned cravats wondered at his—not "obstinacy"; not when there might be a mike even in the corner saloon; say, his "timelessness".

The bright young men became bright young-old men, and the magazine which had been conceived as a vehicle for deadheading house ads of the mail order picture business went into the black. On the cover of every issue of *DEATH* was a pictured execution-of-the-week, and no price for one was ever too high. A fifty-thousand-dollar donation to a mosque had purchased the right to secretly snap the Bread Ordeal by which perished a Yemenite suspected of tapping an oil pipeline. An interminable illustrated History of Flagellation was a staple of the reading matter, and the Medical Section (in color) was tremendously popular. So too was the weekly Traffic Report.

When the last of the Compact Ships was launched into the Pacific the event made *DEATH* because of the several fatal accidents which accompanied the launching; otherwise Merdeka ignored the ships. It was strange that he who had unorthodoxies about everything had no opinion at all about the Compact Ships and their crews. Perhaps it was that he really knew he was the greatest manslayer who ever lived, and even so could not face commanding total extinction, including that of the seaborne leaven. The more articulate Sokei-an, who in the name of Rinzei Zen Buddhism was at that time depopulating the immense area dominated by China, made no bones about it: "Even I in my Hate may err; let the celestial vessels be." The opinions of Dr. Spät, European member of the trio, are forever beyond recovery due to his advocacy of the "one-generation" plan.

With advancing years Merdeka's wits cooled and gelled. There came a time when he needed a theory and was forced to stab the button of the intercom for his young-old Managing Communicator and growl at him: "Give me a theory!" And the M.C. reeled out: "The structural intermesh of *DEATH: the Weekly Picture Magazine* with Western culture is no random point-event but a rising world-line. Predecessor attitudes such as the Hollywood dogma 'No tits—blood!' and the tabloid press' exploitation of violence were floundering and empirical. It was Merdeka who sigma-ized the convergent traits of our times and asymptotically congruentizes with them publicationwise. Wrestling and the rollerderby as blood sports, the routinization of femicide in the detective tale, the standardization at one million per year of traffic fatalities, the wholesome interest of our youth in gang rumbles, all point toward the Age of Hate and Death. The ethic of Love and Life is obsolescent, and who is to say that Man is the loser thereby? Life and Death compete in the marketplace of ideas for the Mind of Man—"

Merdeka growled something and snapped off the set. Merdeka leaned back. Two billion circulation this week, and the auto ads were beginning to Tip. Last year only the suggestion of a dropped shopping basket as the Dynajetic 16 roared across the page, this year a hand, limp on the pictured pavement. Next year, blood. In February the Sylphella Salon chain ads had Tipped, with a crash. "—and the free optional judo course for slenderized Madame or Mademoiselle: learn how to kill a man with your lovely bare hands, with or without mess as desired." Applications had risen 28 per cent. By *God* there was a structural intermesh for you!

It was too slow; it was still too slow. He picked up a direct-line phone and screamed into it: "Too slow! What am I paying you people for? The world is wallowing in filth! Movies are dirtier than ever! Kissing! Pawing! Ogling! Men and women together—obscene! Clean up the magazine covers! Clean up the ads!"

The person at the other end of the direct line was Executive Secretary of the Society for Purity in Communications; Merdeka had no need to announce himself to him, for Merdeka was S.P.C.'s principal underwriter. He began to rattle off at once: "We've got the Mothers' March on Washington this week, sir, and a mass dummy pornographic mailing addressed to every Middle Atlantic State female between the ages of six and twelve next week, sir; I believe this one-two punch will put the Federal Censorship Commission over the goal line before recess—"

Merdeka hung up. "Lewd communications," he snarled. "Breeding, breeding, breeding, like maggots in a garbage can. Burning and breeding. But we will make them clean."

He did not need a Theory to tell him that he could not take away Love without providing a substitute.

He walked down Sixth Avenue that night, for the first time in years. In this saloon he had argued; outside that saloon he had been punched in the nose. Well, he was winning the argument, all the arguments. A mother and daughter walked past uneasily, eyes on the shadows. The mother was dressed

Square; she wore a sheath dress that showed her neck and clavicles at the top and her legs from mid-shin at the bottom. In some parts of town she'd be spat on, but the daughter, never. The girl was Hip; she was covered from neck to ankles by a loose, unbelted sack-culotte. Her mother's hair floated; hers was hidden by a cloche. Nevertheless the both of them were abruptly yanked into one of those shadows they prudently had eyed, for they had not watched the well-lit sidewalk for waiting nooses.

The familiar sounds of a Working Over came from the shadows as Merdeka strolled on. "I mean cool!" an ecstatic young voice—boy's, girl's, what did it matter?—breathed between crunching blows.

That year the Federal Censorship Commission was created, and the next year the old Internment Camps in the southwest were filled to capacity by violators, and the next year the First Church of Merdeka was founded in Chicago. Merdeka died of an aortal aneurism five years after that, but his soul went marching on.

—V—

"The Family that Prays together Slays together", was the wall-motto in the apartment, but there was no evidence that the implied injunction had been observed. The bedroom of the mother and the father were secured by steel doors and terrific locks, but Junior had got them all the same; somehow he had burned through the steel.

"Thermite?" Jewel Flyte asked herself softly, trying to remember. First he had got the father, quickly and quietly with a wire garotte as he lay sleeping, so as not to alarm his mother. To her he had taken her own spiked knobkerry and got in a mortal stroke, but not before she reached under her pillow for a pistol. Junior's teen-age bones testified by their arrangement to the violence of that leaden blow.

Incredulously they looked at the family library of comic books, published in a series called "The Merdekan Five-Foot Shelf of Classics". Jewel Flyte leafed slowly through one called *Moby Dick* and found that it consisted of a near-braining in a bedroom, agonizingly-depicted deaths at sea, and for a climax the eating alive of one Ahab by a monster. "Surely there must have been more," she whispered.

Chaplain Pendleton put down *Hamlet* quickly and held onto a wall. He was quite sure that he felt his sanity slipping palpably away, that he would gibber in a moment. He prayed and after a while felt better; he rigorously kept his eyes away from the Classics after that.

Mrs. Graves snorted at the waste of it all, at the picture of the ugly, pop-eyed, busted-nose man labeled MERDEKA THE CHOSEN, THE PURE, THE PURIFIER. There were *two* tables, which was a folly. Who needed two tables? Then she looked closer, saw that one of them was really a blood-stained flogging bench and felt slightly ill. Its name-plate said *Correctional Furniture Corp. Size 6, Ages 10-14.* She had, God knew, slapped her children more than once when they deviated from her standard of perfection, but when she saw those stains she felt a stirring of warmth for the parricidal bones in the next room.

Captain Salter said: "Let's get organized. Does anybody think there are any of them left?"

"I think not," said Mrs. Graves. "People like that can't survive. The world must have been swept clean. They, ah, killed one another but that's not the important point. This couple had one child, age ten to fourteen. This cabin of theirs seems to be built for one child. We should look at a few more cabins to learn whether a one-child family is—was—normal. If we find out that it was, we can suspect that they are—gone. Or nearly so." She coined a happy phrase: "By race suicide."

"The arithmetic of it is quite plausible," Salter said. "If no factors work except the single-child factor, in one century of five generations a population of two billion will have bred itself down to 125 million. In another century, the population is just under four million. In another, 122 thousand . . . by the thirty-second generation the last couple descended from the original two billion will breed one child, and that's the end. And there are the other factors. Besides those who do not breed by choice—" His eyes avoided Jewel Flyte. "—there are the things we have seen on the stairs, and in the corridor, and in these compartments."

"Then there's our answer," said Mrs. Graves. She smacked the obscene table with her hand, forgetting what it was. "We beach the ship and march the ship's company onto dry land. We clean up, we learn what we have to to get along—" Her words trailed off. She shook her head. "Sorry," she said gloomily. "I'm talking nonsense."

The chaplain understood her, but he said: "The land is merely another of the many mansions. Surely they could learn!"

"It's not politically feasible," Salter said. "Not in its present form." He thought of presenting the proposal to the Ship's Council in the shadow of the mast that bore The Compact, and twitched his head in an involuntary negative.

"There is a formula possible," Jewel Flyte said.

The Brownells burst in on them then, all eighteen of the Brownells. They had been stalking the shore party since its landing. Nine sack-culotted women in cloches and nine men in penitential black, they streamed through the gaping door and surrounded the sea people with a ring of spears. Other factors had indeed operated, but this was not yet the thirty-second generation of extinction.

The leader of the Brownells, a male, said with satisfaction: "Just when we needed new blood." Salter understood that he was not speaking in genetic terms.

The females, more verbal types, said critically: "Whores, obviously. Displaying their limbs without shame, brazenly flaunting the rotted pillars of the temple of lust. Come from the accursed sea itself, abode of infamy, to seduce us from our decent and regular lives."

"We know what to do with the women," said the male leader. The rest took up the antiphon.

"We'll knock them down."

"And roll them on their backs."

"And pull one arm out and tie it fast."

"And pull the other arm out and tie it fast."

"And pull one limb out and tie it fast."

"And pull the other limb out and tie it fast."

"And then—"

"We'll beat them to death and Merdeka will smile."

Chaplain Pemberton stared incredulously. "You must look into your hearts," he told them in a reasonable voice. "You must look deeper than you have, and you will find that you have been deluded. This is not the way for human beings to act. Somebody has misled you dreadfully. Let me explain—"

"Blasphemy," the leader of the females said, and put her spear expertly into the chaplain's intestines. The shock of the broad, cold blade pulsed through him and felled him. Jewel Flyte knelt beside him instantly, checking heart beat and breathing. He was alive.

"Get up," the male leader said. "Displaying and offering yourself to such as we is useless. We are pure in heart."

A male child ran to the door. "Wagners!" he screamed. "Twenty Wagners coming up the stairs!"

His father roared at him: "Stand straight and don't mumble!" and slashed out with the butt of his spear, catching him hard in the ribs. The child grinned, but only after the pure-hearted eighteen had run to the stairs.

Then he blasted a whistle down the corridor while the sea-people stared with what attention they could divert from the bleeding chaplain. Six doors popped open at the whistle and men and women emerged from them to launch spears into the backs of the Brownells clustered to defend the stairs. "Thanks, pop!" the boy kept screaming while the pure-hearted Wagners swarmed over the remnants of the pure-hearted Brownells; at last his screaming bothered one of the Wagners and the boy was himself speared.

Jewel Flyte said: "I've had enough of this. Captain, please pick the chaplain up and come along."

"They'll kill us."

"You'll have the chaplain," said Mrs. Graves. "One moment." She darted into a bedroom and came back hefting the spiked knobkerry.

"Well, perhaps," the girl said. She began undoing the long row of buttons down the front of her coveralls and shrugged out of the garment, then unfastened and stepped out of her underwear. With the clothes over her arm she walked into the corridor and to the stairs, the stupefied captain and inspector following.

To the pure-hearted Merkdeans she was not Phryne winning her case; she was Evil incarnate. They screamed, broke and ran wildly, dropping their weapons. That a human being could do such a thing was beyond their comprehension; Merdeka alone knew what kind of monster this was that drew them strangely and horribly, in violation of all sanity. They ran as she had hoped they would; the other side of the coin was spearing even more swift and thorough than would have been accorded to her fully clothed. But they ran, gibbering with fright and covering their eyes, into apartments and corners of the corridor, their back turned on the awful thing.

The sea-people picked their way over the shambles at the stairway and went unopposed down the stairs and to the dock. It was a troublesome piece of work for Salter to pass the chaplain down to Mrs. Graves in the boat, but in ten minutes they had cast off, rowed out a little and set sail to catch the land breeze generated by the differential twilight cooling of water and brick. After playing her part in stepping the mast, Jewel Flyte dressed.

"It won't always be that easy," she said when the last button was fastened. Mrs. Graves had been thinking the same thing, but had not said it to avoid the appearance of envying that superb young body.

Salter was checking the chaplain as well as he knew how. "I think he'll be all right," he said. "Surgical repair and a long rest. He hasn't lost much blood. This is a strange story we'll have to tell the Ship's Council."

Mrs. Graves said: "They've no choice. We've lost our net and the land is there waiting for us. A few maniacs oppose us—what of it?"

Again a huge fish lazily surfaced; Salter regarded it thoughtfully. He said: "They'll propose scavenging bronze ashore and fashioning another net and going on just as if nothing had happened. And really, we could do that, you know."

Jewel Flyte said: "No. Not forever. This time it was the net, at the end of harvest. What if it were three masts in midwinter, in mid-Atlantic?"

"Or," said the captain, "the rudder—any time. Anywhere. But can you imagine telling the Council they've got to walk off the ship onto land, take up quarters in those brick cabins, change *everything?* And fight maniacs, and learn to *farm?"*

"There must be a way," said Jewel Flyte. "Just as Merdeka, whatever it was, was a way. There were too many people, and Merdeka was the answer to too many people. There's always an answer. Man is a land mammal in spite of brief excursions at sea. We were seed stock put aside, waiting for the land to be cleared so we could return. Just as these offshore fish are waiting very patiently for us to stop harvesting twice a year so they can return to deep water and multiply. What's the way, captain?"

He thought hard. "We could," he said slowly, "begin by simply sailing in close and fishing the offshore waters for big stuff. Then tie up and build a sort of bridge from the ship to the shore. We'd continue to live aboard the ship but we'd go out during daylight to try farming."

"It sounds right."

"And keep improving the bridge, making it more and more solid, until before they notice it it's really a solid part of the ship and a solid part of the shore. It might take . . . mmm . . . ten years?"

"Time enough for the old shellbacks to make up their minds," Mrs. Graves unexpectedly snorted.

"And we'd relax the one-to-one reproduction rule, and some young adults will simply be crowded over the bridge to live on the land—" His face suddenly fell. "And then the whole damned farce starts all over again, I suppose. I pointed out that it takes thirty-two generations bearing one child apiece to run a population of two billion into zero. Well, I should have mentioned that it takes thirty-two generations bearing four children apiece to run a population of two into two billion. Oh, what's the use, Jewel?"

She chuckled. "There was an answer last time," she said. "There will be an answer the next time."

"It won't be the same answer as Merdeka," he vowed. "We grew up a little at sea. This time we can do it with brains and not with nightmares and superstition."

"I don't know," she said. "Our ship will be the first, and then the other ships will have their accidents one by one and come and tie up and build their bridges hating every minute of it for the first two generations and then not hating it, just living it . . . and who will be the greatest man who ever lived?"

The captain looked horrified.

"Yes, you! Salter, the Builder of the Bridge; Tommy, do you know an old word for 'bridge-builder'? *Pontifex."*

"Oh, my God!" Tommy Salter said in despair.

A flicker of consciousness was passing through the wounded chaplain; he heard the words and was pleased that somebody aboard was praying.

N.B.

The withdrawal of American News Company from magazine distribution last year caused a lot of confusion on the newsstands, some of which is still with us — as witness recent testimony to that effect from our respected colleagues, *Galaxy* and *F&SF*.

Vanguard's distributor is one of the biggest remaining in business, and we expect to get good service from him; but neither he nor anyone else can absolutely guarantee that Vanguard will be on your local newsstand regularly. The situation is still too shifty to make such guarantees possible.

The moral: You'd better subscribe. Rates are $6.00 for 20 issues in the United States, $6.50 a year in Canada, $7.00 elsewhere. And just to prove that we mean business, we can give you a lifetime subscription (offer limited to the first three issues; after that, it will be withdrawn) for $25. Care to bet $25 that you'll live longer than we will? And for a limited time only, we are making a special offer of a Spoken Arts record. See inside front cover for details.

COMING NEXT ISSUE

MINE HOST, MINE ADVERSARY by Lester del Rey is our lead novelette for next issue, again with a cover by Ed Emsh. Written with del Rey's characteristic combination of tough-mindedness and depth of feeling, it's a story you won't forget. Also featured will be MIRROR, MIRROR by Alan E. Nourse, a disturbing novelette dealing with an invasion of Saturn — of all places. The short stories will include TO BE CONTINUED by Damon Knight, an unusual blend of time travel and time-building; ALONE by A. Bertram Chandler, a powerful study of the first man to be fired into deep space.

The Fiction House Press Replica Line is available at www.FictionHousePress.com

Continued from BACK COVER

YES, TAKE ANY THREE of these exciting books—worth up to $10.95 in publishers' editions—yours for only $1 simply by joining this new kind of book club NOW. They're all masterworks of science-fiction (or factual science books of special interest to science-fiction fans), by top-flight authors. And they're loaded with rocket-fast reading that takes you soaring through time and space. All in handsomely bound library editions you'll be proud to own! Choose ANY 3 and mail coupon below—without money—TODAY!

SEND NO MONEY—*Just Mail Coupon*

Indicate on coupon your choice of any 3 of the new science-fiction masterpieces described here. One will be considered your first selection, for which you'll be billed only $1 plus a few cents postage. The other TWO are yours FREE as a membership GIFT. Every month you will be offered the cream of the new $2.50 to $3.75 science-fiction books — for only $1 each. (Occasionally an *extra-value* selection is offered which, because of its large size and importance will be priced slightly higher.) But you take *only* those books you really want—as few as 4 a year. This offer may be withdrawn at any time. So mail the coupon RIGHT NOW to:

SCIENCE-FICTION BOOK CLUB
Dept. 8VSF-6
Garden City, N. Y.

THE NAKED SUN by Isaac Asimov. For description, please see other side. (Pub. ed. $2.95).

THE BEST FROM FANTASY AND SCIENCE-FICTION. (New Edition) 17 thrilling stories selected from *Fantasy and Science-Fiction Magazine*. Adventure in other worlds . . . mystery, intrigue, suspense! (Pub. ed. $3.50).

OMNIBUS OF SCIENCE-FICTION. 43 classic stories by top authors. Wonders of Earth and Man. Amazing inventions. Space Travel and Visitors from Outer Space. Adventures in Dimension. Worlds of Tomorrow. (Pub. ed. $3.50).

TREASURY OF SCIENCE-FICTION CLASSICS. 4 famous novels; a complete play; scores of all-time great S-F stories, including H. G. Wells' "Invasion from Mars," made famous by Orsen Welles' hoax newscast. (Pub. ed. $2.95).

THE ASTOUNDING SCIENCE-FICTION ANTHOLOGY. A story about the first A-bomb . . . written BEFORE it was invented! Plus a score of other best tales from a dozen years of Astounding Science-Fiction Magazine (Pub. ed. $3.50).

SATELLITE! by Erik Bergaust & William Beller. Top experts reveal full FACTS on the first man-made Satellite — information not even available in technical journals! (Pub. ed. $3.95).

SCIENCE-FICTION BOOK CLUB,
Dept. 8VSF-6, Garden City, N. Y.

Rush the 3 books checked below and enroll me as a member. One is my first selection, for which you may bill me $1 plus a few cents postage. The other 2 are FREE as a membership GIFT. Every month send the club's free bulletin, describing coming selections. For each book I accept, I will pay only $1 plus shipping. (Occasional extra-value selection at a slightly higher price.) But I need take only 4 books during the year and may resign at any time after that.

GUARANTEE: If not delighted, I may return books in 7 days, pay nothing; membership will be cancelled.

- ☐ **Astounding S-F Anthology**
- ☐ **Best from Fantasy and Science-Fiction**
- ☐ **The Naked Sun**
- ☐ **Omnibus of Science-Fiction**
- ☐ **Satellite!**
- ☐ **Treasury of S-F Classics**

Name ______________________________

Address ______________________________

S61

City ____________ **Zone** ______ **State** ____________

Same offer in CANADA. Address 105 Bond Street, Toronto 2. (Offer good only in U. S. A. and Canada.)

www.ingramcontent.com/pod-product-compliance
Lightning Source LLC
LaVergne TN
LVHW091005080826
845145LV00003B/1132

* 9 7 8 1 6 4 7 2 0 4 0 0 6 *